One Hun(
By Frank B

1

There was a boy who lived alone in a hundred-storey tower block in the Dirty City. His name was Lester.

Lester didn't know his neighbours, but he imagined them. Each day he'd compose no less than one hundred stories.

The stories had titles such as *The Girl Who Vomited Cash* and *The Man Who Had Conversations With Concepts*.

His favourite story was about himself. It was called *The Boy Who Sweated Music*.

It went:

There was a boy who sweated music. His name was Lester. He lived alone in a tower block in the Dirty City. The tower had one hundred storeys.

He woke up one morning to the sound of an offbeat rhythm.

The rhythm was an independent being. It had its own philosophy – its own ideas about what music was supposed to be. It was a Master of Arts and Sciences. It had rewritten the periodic table with reams of newly-discovered elements. It had devised its own beat formations.

Beats throbbed through the boy's body.

He pulled the duvet off.

The beats pounded louder. They swarmed around the room, through cracks in the ceiling and down the rusty ventilation shaft.

From above and below came the noise from the neighbours. Some of them sang. Some of them shrieked.

The bass kicked in.

Lester whipped off his t-shirt. A further blast of sound escaped from his chest, closely resembling violins, but without an actual instrument attached.

Below and above, the neighbours stomped, as though stomping were their only option.

Lester floated several feet above the mattress.

The strings soared into the first of several crescendos.

He crawled across the ceiling to the window.

Once out in the breeze, he observed the view below him. The city was heavenly and hideous.

He broke into breast stroke as he swooped higher. The music was muffled by the atmosphere but the neighbours still heard, and continued dancing, even when Lester disappeared into the clouds.

No one ever saw him again.

They spoke about that day for years. They told their kids, their nieces and their third cousins.

Eventually most of the people who were there began to doubt it had happened at all. But still, at the back of their heads the beats and bass boomed on and on…

2

There was a girl who vomited cash. The first time it happened she blocked the drain.

"I dropped my wallet," she explained to the plumber. It would prove to be the first of many casual deceptions.

Retching steel and copper up her throat was excruciating, but impossible to resist.

She'd binge at the city's most expensive restaurants and spew the coins into a paper bag as payment.

Her boyfriend asked why she was so ill and so rich. She refused to answer either question, even when she grew iller and richer.

"It doesn't matter," was her only response.

Pretty soon, forcing herself to throw up became too much to bear. Besides, she was rich enough to last the rest of her life without working, which suited her fine.

Her real passion was painting. She painted pictures with eccentric titles like *Dog's Un-Dogginess to Dog*, *The Twelve Lives of Adrian* and *The Human Stacking Doll*. By her own admission she was a terrible painter, but that didn't matter.

"Nothing matters," she told herself.

Then she fell pregnant. With morning sickness, more Dirty City dollars arrived. She put them in a savings account for the foetus.

She left her boyfriend, who'd been asking far too many questions. From that point on, life was all about her and her child.

She had her daughter's name inscribed on her chest. She swore it was the only tattoo she'd ever need.

She remained a devoted mother but friends and family saw her plunge into a private despair. She had enough cash to buy her own building but she remained in her tiny apartment in a tower block.

She never explained why she was unhappy. It may have been irrational, but she saw herself as a living metaphor for the city's financial crisis.

"I'm sorry," she told her child. "I know you don't understand what I'm saying, but you're the only person I can talk to. The funny thing is, I don't understand either. I don't know why I vomit cash. Perhaps there isn't a reason."

Her sister visited for the weekend and found her on the ground on Saturday morning, her body obliterated on the concrete beside a small puddle of coins. She'd jumped from the hundredth storey.

Her daughter inherited everything, and was destined to grow up not remembering her mother. Her relatives said it was probably just as well.

The economy picked up the following year.

3

There was a girl who was born with four girls inside her. They called her the Human Stacking Doll.

The phenomenon was identified while she was still in the womb. Doctors marvelled at the sight of five separate layers of flesh and skin, each sharing the same organs and skeleton, yet each an independent being.

Her parents told her she was special. *Everyone's parents say that*, she thought.

She was a clumsy teenager. Then she discovered cider.

After a party at a friend's house, she tripped over the doormat on the way out, falling head first onto the driveway.

When her friends tried to pull her up, they found themselves tearing off the skin on her shoulders like her body were a reel of cellophane.

Before her friends had chance to be horrified, the Human Stacking Doll climbed to her feet. Her clothes fell off. She removed her scalp and peeled off her face.

"That's better," said the second girl.

In one joyous swoop of the arm, she ripped off the remainder of her outer layer.

"Can someone get me some clothes?" she said. "It's freezing out here."

The new girl was a little more responsible than her predecessor. She studied law, passing her bar exam at the age of nineteen. On the night of her graduation, she was hit by a speeding cyclist. Her flesh was virtually obliterated.

The third girl had no interest in law. She ditched her new qualification, choosing instead to pursue a career as a paragliding instructor. She didn't last long.

The forth girl was surprised none of her predecessors had been tempted to achieve fame and fortune by drawing public attention to their unique physiology. Once the press got hold of the story, she became a celebrity overnight. She was the subject of no less than fourteen TV documentaries. She published seven volumes of autobiography in the space of three years.

It wasn't long before the constant media attention made her pine for her older, simpler life. She sold her house in the country and rented the flat in a tower block which she'd stayed in as a student. She remained indoors with the curtains drawn for weeks. No one knew where she'd disappeared to – not even her family.

After buying a magazine as part of her online shopping order, she found her face printed on the cover alongside the caption: "Whatever happened to the Human Stacking Doll?"

Good question, she thought.

That night, she drew back the curtains, opened the window and climbed out onto the grubby ledge.

"My parents said I was special," she said, "but everyone's parents say that."

She jumped into the icy air. She was fifty seven floors up.

A matter of seconds later, a cry erupted from the ground. The final girl emerged from her shattered sibling's remains. She was a little over three feet tall.

"Finally!" she cried at the windows above.

Her head span in circles, as she marvelled at the city lights, seeing the world for the first time as a person in her own right.

"Are you alright?" said a voice. She turned to see a wide-eyed passerby, crouching down to her level. He looked directly in her eyes as a means of distracting his attention from the messy remains of her sister.

"More than alright," she said.

"What happened?"

"I released myself."

"Hang on – you're not…?"

The Human Stacking Doll nodded. "There's just one of me now – the final piece of the jigsaw."

The passerby closed his eyes and placed his hand on her shoulder. "I guess this means you've lost four sisters," he said quietly.

"It's alright," she said. "Who do you think killed them in the first place? Who's been the demon within, pulling the strings, helping them make their horrendous decisions?"

The passerby removed his hand from her shoulder. "So, what are you going to do now?" he said.

"I don't know," she said. "There are so many things I've never done. I've never eaten ice cream, or performed a somersault, or ran through a storm with the wind in my face. I've got a lot of catching up to do."

The passerby decided to direct his gaze at the mess on the ground rather than face the Human Stacking Doll's maniacal smile.

Unable to look at the ground either, he raised his head again.

By that point, she'd already vanished into the dark.

4

There was a hundred-storey tower block located on the outskirts of the Dirty City. Her name was Jennifer.

She was by far the tallest building in the area. Years ago, plans had been drawn up to build a large cluster of towers of a similar height. The plans were cancelled, shortly after the neighbouring buildings were bulldozed. Consequently, Jennifer was the only building within a mile's radius. She was surrounded on all sides by an expanse of flat, featureless concrete.

The only other enormous buildings in sight were located in the central district known as the Clean City.

Jennifer was the only skyscraper the tourists didn't photograph. She was the city's exiled second-cousin; a monumental black sheep.

Jennifer didn't care.

That's not to say she didn't have feelings. She had her own beliefs and opinions. She preferred drum and bass to dubstep. She preferred the sword-swallower in apartment 438 to the accountant in 439.

Her ever-changing personality was made up of the residual brainwave energy of her thousand inhabitants. She had the intelligence of a super-computer combined with an incalculable emotional capacity.

Only one of the tower block's inhabitants operated entirely independently of this gargantuan mind: a boy named Lester.

Jennifer wasn't bothered by Lester at first. "I'm a giant rectangular brain," she reminded herself. "I can explore every avenue of every single mind that makes up my own. Why should I care about a single unexplained stray?"

One day, however, Jennifer's curiosity got the better of her.

Lester was sitting by his window watching the clouds.

"Hello Lester," said Jennifer.

"Hello," said Lester.

"You're not surprised I'm talking to you?"

"Why would I be?"

"Do you know who I am?"

"Yes. You're the building. What can I do for you?"

"I was just wondering ... well, I apologise about this, but I've been watching you."

"I see," said Lester.

"I can't help noticing there's something different about you," said Jennifer. "You don't have a TV or a computer or a phone. You don't listen to music. You don't even read books."

"I don't need to," said Lester.

"Why?" said Jennifer.

"Why do you want to know?"

"I suppose I want to know what goes on in your head."

Lester considered the question. Several hours passed. The clouds turned black.

"I invent things," he said.

"Huh?" said Jennifer. "Sorry, half of me's asleep. What did you say?"

"I said, I invent things. Stories."

"Stories," said Jennifer thoughtfully. "Yes. That's what I want. I'm glad I spoke to you, Lester. Tell me a story."

"Why?"

"Because I need one."

"Why?"

"Because I know everything there is to know. I'm sitting here with the combined knowledge of everyone who's ever entered me. I want to hear something I don't know. I want to be surprised."

"I don't really share my stories with other people," said Lester.

"I'm not a person," said Jennifer.

"OK. Maybe I'll make you an exception."

"Great. Go ahead."

"Wait a moment," said Lester. "I'm trying to create something that'd appeal to you."

"Thank you," said Jennifer. "Just tell me when you're ready."

"I'm ready," said Lester.

"What's the story called?"

"It's three stories really," said Lester. "They're called *The Ghosts of Buildings*."

5

There was a tour guide operating at night across the empty space between Jennifer and the city. His tour was called *The Ghosts of Buildings*.

The guide didn't advertise, and any passersby who somehow found their way onto the tour were politely dissuaded from telling their friends.

"You can't have a secret that isn't a secret," he'd whisper.

Most evenings no one would turn up at all, but the guide conducted the tour anyway, muttering his meticulously-prepared script into the darkness.

One evening a boy arrived. He was the first person to have attended the tour for several weeks.

"What are you doing here?" said the guide.

"I'm here for the tour," said the boy.

"What tour?"

"You mean there isn't one?"

The guide rolled his eyes in a perfect three-sixty circle. "How do you know?" he said.

"I saw you yesterday. Sorry to be impolite, but I eavesdropped a bit. I didn't hear much but it sounded interesting."

"Interesting, eh?" said the guide thoughtfully.

"Yes."

"Well, we'd better begin. What's your name, sir?"

"Lester."

"OK. As I'm sure you're aware, Lester, when a building dies, it leaves a mark in the space it once occupied. More than a mark, in fact. You know how many buildings were demolished to make way for the abandoned skyscrapers, Lester?"

"No."

"Two hundred and forty five."

Lester looked around the blank concrete sheet, attempting to imagine two hundred and forty five buildings crammed into it.

"Two hundred and forty-five," the guide repeated. "And every single one of them remains impeccably alive."

They walked a mile, weaving their way in and out of invisible alleyways. Every so often, the guide would point upwards, etching a dead building's outline with his fingertip.

For a while, Lester suspected the guide was going to recount the story of every single one of them – houses, barbers shops, places of worship. Thankfully, they stepped up the pace once they got closer to Jennifer.

"And now for the finale," said the guide, pointing upwards.

"That's Jennifer," said Lester. "I live there."

"I'm not pointing at Jennifer," said the guide. "I'm pointing beside her – there, there and there. The bulldozed ghosts are present in some small quiet way, but the essence of the buildings that never existed is far more pervasive."

Lester stared ahead, examining the empty space beside his home. "How can something that never existed have an essence?" he said.

"Ever wondered where ideas go when they die?"

"Yes," said Lester. "I've often wondered that."

"The answer is, they hang around waiting to be rediscovered. Or perhaps they're not waiting for anything – they're just *existing*. Some abandoned ideas are little more than whispers in the night. Others, like the great towering concepts to our left and right, scream out through the empty space. The building you live in, Lester, has a multitude of unborn brothers and sisters. The economic boom promised massive levels of investment in this area. The city was promised huge apartment blocks, offices, hotels, shopping malls. It would be cleaner than the Clean City itself. Only one of these buildings was ever built."

"I understand," said Lester.

"There are many stories I could tell," said the guide, "but let's start with The Great Indoors."

"OK."

6

The 75-storey construction known as The Great Indoors was Jennifer's slightly younger and smaller brother. His apartments were inhabited almost exclusively by farmyard animals.

The city's unique experiment in urban farming was proposed as a more humane and cost-effective means of rearing livestock. The first twelve floors were occupied by sheep. Pigs were floors 13-27. Poultry were above them, then cattle.

The top eight floors were occupied by the farmers themselves – not that they did much work. It was amazing how adaptable the creatures were when it came to operating their own kitchens, bathrooms and sleeping areas when given the opportunity.

Occasionally a bull would break his way out through the fire exit and fume his way through the streets. Local police were equipped with electric rods to cover for this eventuality.

On one such occasion, a bull managed to creep down the stairs at three in the morning. He gazed in wonder at the half-built skyscrapers that surrounded him. The bull crept in and out of the city's labyrinth of alleyways working his way further and further away from home.

Heading in the direction of the curious rushing noises and bright lights in the distance, the bull eventually found himself at Dirty City Airport. Despite the unsociable hour, the bull encountered a phenomenal buzz of activity. His plan was to behave as inconspicuously as possible so as not to be recognised as a bull. He crept along the concourse, taking in the sights. His attention was drawn to the escalators. He jumped aboard, behind a pair of tourists. Their suitcase was slightly larger than he was.

The bull had seen some spectacular sights through his apartment window over the years, but he could never have conceived of a contraption that allowed you to travel upstairs while standing still. Forget planes – this was the most awesome invention he'd ever encountered.

He jumped instinctively when he reached the top, successfully dismounting.

He continued wandering the complex, on the hunt for more escalators.

He discovered something even more intriguing: a *moving walkway*.

The bull approached the walkway, tentatively. His front legs jerked forward faster than his back legs could keep up with. Somehow he managed to remain vertical.

He glided forward. A queue of tourists waited patiently behind.

Seemingly getting the hang of this mysterious machine, the bull jumped off at the other end. He immediately headed for the walkway heading in the opposite direction.

After forty or fifty circuits, the bull decided that was enough merriment for one evening.

He left the airport and wove his way back through the labyrinth of alleyways until he arrived home. He climbed the fire escape and busted his way through his apartment door. He was asleep before his head had hit the carpet.

Deprived of language, the bull would never be able to tell anyone about the journey he'd taken. It didn't matter.

A couple of hours later, having checked their enormous suitcase onto their flight, one tourist turned to the other and said, "Funny thing ... did you notice that guy who was standing behind us earlier?"

"Yeah, that was a bit odd now you come to mention it."

"Was I seeing things, or did he have *horns?*"

7

Next door to The Great Indoors stood the tallest and slimmest building in the city: The Haddock. As the name suggests, The Haddock was a skyscraper in the shape of a giant fish. With its tail to the ground, the tip of the Haddock's nose constituted the city's highest point. Its eyes were observatories from which the stars and the city below could be examined in the finest possible detail.

The Haddock's interior was laid out in the shape of a skeleton. The building didn't have apartments – it had bone-shaped bunks, branching off from the central elevator shaft running up and down The Haddock's spine. The communal kitchens, bathrooms and recreational areas were based on the expansive ground floor just below the tail.

Critics said it was never going to work. Essentially, The Haddock was a house-share for five hundred people. Imagine the arguments. It only takes one anti-social animal clogging up the bathroom sink and hogging the remote control to ruin the whole thing for everyone.

As it happened, the living arrangements worked out incredibly well. Communal areas were kept clean and tidy because the alternatives were unthinkable for everyone. You couldn't just leave the washing up unless you wanted a mountain of dirty plates. There were enough hands to pitch in.

Consequently, The Haddock's residents were forced to get along with each other. A feeling of unheard-of community spirit emerged, infecting them with an incurable case of contentment.

The Haddock's reputation quickly spread. The waiting list for bunk-space reached tens of thousands.

Before long, replica buildings were constructed – The Salmon, The Sole, The Halibut, and so on.

A hundred years later, virtually every building in the city was constructed in the shape of a fish.

The Dirty City was no longer known as The Dirty City. They called it The Shoal.

8

"I don't suppose you know too much about the architect who designed these buildings?" said the guide.

"No," said Lester. "People don't usually tell me things."

"Well, let's start at the beginning – or, rather, the end."

"OK."

#

Fritz Deep was a mysterious figure. Everyone in the industry knew his name but very few had the privilege of meeting him face to face.

Deep was responsible for the most daring works of architecture in the Clean City. He built The Canvas, The Strawberry and The Biggest Clock in the World. When plans to develop the Dirty City arose, he insisted on setting up camp in the site. He was, in fact, the first person to live in Jennifer. She was just two storeys at the time. In order to fully immerse himself in his work, Deep needed to be as close as possible to the land in which his creations would be rooted.

He soundproofed the room to block out the noise of the construction workers above and below. He didn't leave the apartment for weeks. By all accounts, he spent the entirety of the day staring intently out of the window.

One afternoon he was visited by Jeremy Mercer, a Member of Parliament who liked to think of himself as one of the key figures in the Dirty City's redevelopment.

"It's an honour to meet you," said Mercer.

"Mmmm," said Deep thoughtfully. "Honour. Yes."

"We're all very excited about this project."

"Mmmm ... Yes ... Excited."

"I'm just wondering how the plans are going."

Deep's face was as empty as the walls. "What plans?"

The politician's face spasmed momentarily. "The plans you've been working on for the past few weeks," he said.

"Oh," said Deep. "I haven't actually started yet."

"Then what've you been doing?"

"Getting a feel for the place, really."

"Do you think you might make a start at some point?"

Deep's eyes examined the ceiling for a moment. "If it means that much to you, I could rush through the remainder of my "getting a feel" time. Give me a couple of weeks."

Mercer returned two weeks later.

"Well?" he said. "Do you have a "feel for the place" now, Mr Deep?"

"Not yet," said Deep. "Sorry. There's something special here, but I can't for the life of me work out what it is. Give me another two weeks."

Two weeks passed.

"Have you figured it out yet?" said Mercer.

"Give me another two weeks."

A fortnight later:

"Surely you have news for me now."

"I have news," said Deep, "but I'm not sure it's the news you want to hear."

"Any news is good news," said Mercer.

"OK," said Deep. "My news is, I need another two weeks."

This process continued for two years. Every fortnight, Mercer returned to find Deep sitting in an empty room having completed zero percent of his work. By this point, Jennifer was complete, and her apartments were being filled.

On his 52nd visit, Mercer didn't bother knocking. He charged through the unlocked door.

"Do you know how many times you've told me to come back in two weeks?" he said.

"Fifty two, I believe," said Deep.

"And still you've done nothing. We've paid you an astronomical fee to brew in this apartment for two whole years. An entire city has put its life on hold while you sit staring out of the window. Well, now you're officially in breach of contract. Our agreement states that the plans must be finished by today. I'm a lenient man, Mr Deep, but if you think you're getting an extension you're every bit as deluded as I think you are. You're officially off the project. Good day."

"Hang on," said Deep. "As it happens, I think I've finally sussed this place out."

"It's too late, Mr Deep. Today's your deadline."

"Surely I'm not officially off the project until the *end* of the day. I'll be done by 5pm."

"I'll believe that when I see it."

Mercer returned to the apartment later that day to find half a tree's worth of paper stacked up on the carpet.

"Care to take a look?" said Deep.

"I might need a summary," said Mercer.

Deep pulled out the relevant bits of paper and presented the politician with one astounding work of architecture after another.

Mercer struggled to control his breathing. Somehow, each individual sketch had made his life better in some unknown way.

"And now," said Deep, "for the *magnum opus*. I call it The Raft."

"Why?"

"Because it floats."

"Floats?"

"Hovers, actually. About a hundred feet off the ground."

"Mr Deep, I suspect you've been cooped up in this room for too long. Buildings don't just *hover*."

Deep handed over his final piece of paper.

Mercer examined the diagram for some time. "Yes," he said after a while. "Of course." It had taken him a minute or two to figure out the science behind Deep's proposition, but once it had sunk in, Mercer wondered why something so simple had never occurred to anyone else.

"Such a shame," he said.

"What's that?"

"It's a shame none of these buildings will ever be constructed."

"What do you mean?"

"As I say, Mr Deep, you've been encased within these walls for too long. The stock market crashed a year and a half ago. The project is long gone."

Deep didn't appear surprised. "So, why didn't you tell me?" he said quietly.

Mercer's face was a perfect picture of smugness. "Ha! It looks like you're not the only one who keeps people waiting."

"Hmmm," said Deep thoughtfully.

Mercer's smile vanished as he realised Deep was in no way upset by him laughing in his face.

"What makes you think I didn't know about the market crash?" said Deep. "About the project being shelved?"

"Not shelved, Mr Deep. *Cancelled.*"

"Whatever term you wish to use. Do you think I wasn't aware of these decisions?"

"By all accounts you haven't left this apartment for two years. You've no internet, no TV, no radio. I expect you don't even know who the Prime Minster is."

"Doesn't mean I'm not perceptive."

"Even so," said Mercer, "if you knew the project was cancelled, why did you stay? Why bother coming up with these ingenious designs when you know they have no future?"

Now it was Deep's turn to be smug. "No future?" he said. "They're here already. They're standing right outside."

Mercer couldn't help peering through the window at the jagged remains of the walls below.

"Can you see them?" said Deep.

"Of course not."

"I'm afraid I told a white lie, Mr Mercer. I haven't just been getting a feel for the place. I've been building. Every brick, every panel, every pane of glass – it's all in place. And look up there, Mr Mercer. Can you see it? The Raft? Floating just next to that cloud?"

"No," said Mercer.

"Not with your eyes," said Deep. "Your *mind*, Mr Mercer. Can you see The Raft?"

Mercer's gaze returned to the piece of paper in his hand. "Yes," he whispered. "Vividly."

Deep beamed at his beautiful, invisible creations. "Build whatever you like here," he said. "Erect more tower blocks, or turn the whole area into a single-storey casino. Or maybe just flatten the whole thing. Whatever happens, Mr Mercer, my creations will still be here. You're looking at the most powerful ideas in the city. Concepts can't be killed, Mr Mercer. Shoot me down dead right now, and those buildings will still be standing. They'll scream out through the coming centuries – Look at me! Look at me!"

"And what about you?" said Mercer.

"I think I'll join them," said Deep.

"I don't understand."

"I've been thinking about ideas," said Deep. "In many ways, they're like children. Once we've given birth to them, they become independent beings. Some do what we ask of them, while others are completely beyond our control. The collection of invisible buildings outside that window belong to the former category. They're my servants. As their creator, I decide when they shrink and when they grow. Living among them would mean ridding myself of people like you, offering opportunities then taking them away, shackling my creativity. Farewell, Mr Mercer."

And with that, Deep was gone. Mercer found himself staring at a blank wall.

"Where are you?" he said.

"Getting ready to move into The Raft," came the reply. "Don't worry, I'll be looking down on you."

"I don't understand," said Mercer. "You can't just vanish into thin air, Mr Deep. Where are you?"

"I'm right here," said Deep. "You can't see me because I'm no longer an architect. I'm an *idea.*"

At that moment, Mercer realised he wasn't hearing the voice through his ears.

For the remainder of the day, and for the rest of his life, Deep's words rang through Mercer's mind like a stranger shouting in the distance.

9

Just before he disappeared into the night, the guide waved his fingers in Lester's face, a centimetre away from jabbing his eyes out. "Don't tell anyone what you've heard today. Not a single person."

"OK," said Lester.

#

"But you've told me?" said Jennifer.

"You said you're not a person," said Lester.

"I just have one question."

"Yeah?"

"Those two people at the end – Deep and Mercer. They're real, right?"

"I don't know," said Lester. "I don't get out much."

"That's a shame."

"Is it?"

Jennifer made one last attempt at cracking open Lester's mind, but the gate remained firmly closed. "I see what you mean," she said.

"Do you?"

"No, not really."

"What are either of us actually talking about?" said Lester.

"Jeremy Mercer," said Jennifer. "I know that he's real. I hear a lot about him. He's rarely in the forefront of anyone's mind, but he's always *there.*"

"Interesting."

"What's interesting," said Jennifer, "is that people *like* him."

"Maybe he's a good politician," said Lester.

"He's a *terrible* politician."

"Or maybe just a good person."

"He's a *terrible* person."

Lester yawned. "Maybe you can tell me about him sometime," he said. "I'm tired."

He lay down on the floor and closed his eyes.

"Goodnight Lester," said Jennifer.

"Goodnight."

10

Due to a series of controversial decisions made early on in his career, Jeremy Mercer was known by many as "The Gardener" – a nickname he'd never been able to shake off, mainly because he had no real interest in what people thought of him. Eventually, he was beaten to death by a cactus.

Mercer's first cabinet post was Environment Minister. Alongside a range of more significant issues, voters regularly wrote to Mercer complaining about the city's overabundance of dandelions. As one pressure group put it: "Dandelions are the scourge of this city. They've invaded our parks, our gardens, the cracks in our pavements. We've petitioned our local councils, who've done less than nothing. It's down to you, Mr Mercer, to yank this weed from its roots once and for all."

Breaking his silence on the subject, Mercer issued a public statement: "Are you people out of your minds? Not only is this so-called "issue" light years outside of my remit, it has no environmental impact whatsoever. If you're going to insist on writing to me, at least pick an important subject like pollution or climate change. I won't necessarily do anything about it, but I'll be less irritated by your correspondence.

"By the way, a weed is merely a successful plant. Want to see the animal kingdom's equivalent of the dandelion? Look in the mirror."

A rival politician wrote an open letter in a leading newspaper, asking: "How long will Mr Mercer continue to write dandelions off as a non-issue? Has he stopped to consider the impact on the tourist industry?"

Mercer responded with a brief open letter of his own: "Fine. Have it your way. Dirty City: say goodbye to your dandelions."

At considerable expense, Mercer arranged for every single unwanted growth to be assaulted by a super virus, killing both the weeds and the soil they grew in.

The following morning, citizens stepped out to discover that in addition to the weeds, every single blade of grass in the city had disappeared.

Mercer had never been one to backtrack when it came to an unpopular policy. This made him rather popular. In a press statement, Mercer stated: "Getting rid of the grass was an accident, but I like it. Green is one of my least favourite colours."

"What steps will be taken to ensure the city's parks and gardens are restored?" asked a journalist.

"None," said Mercer.

There was a short round of applause.

A couple of years later, Mercer returned from an overseas cultural exchange, singing the praises of a city he'd visited in the desert, which was blessed with a maze of gleaming streets and buildings carved from giant slabs of marble. One thing that struck Mercer was the absence of plant life. No trees, no flower beds, just mile after mile of hand-carved shininess, punctuated by the occasional cactus.

Spurred on by his discovery, Mercer immediately ordered the disposal of every single tree in the city.

In response to the public outcry, Mercer stated: "Trees have no place in an urban environment. They clutter up the pavement. They overcrowd the parks. They attract insects, birds and vermin. And the maintenance costs? You'd never believe the figure if I told you. If the public had access to the Government's annual spend on trees, they'd've all been chopped down years ago. Trust me – I'm doing you people a favour."

In the days following the removal of its final tree, the city's remaining plant life chose to commit mass suicide. It was the ultimate act of solidarity. Gardens were left bare and rotting. Empty window boxes were ditched by the side of the street. All that were left were cacti, available in discreet packaging in a quiet corner of a deserted garden centre.

"You may dislike me," said Mercer in a press statement. "I don't blame you. But you clowns voted me in. You're stuck with me for the next two and a half years. Who would you prefer to replace me? Some even bigger imbecile?"

Following Mercer's statement, the Prime Minister made the decision to reshuffle his cabinet, assigning Mercer to a slightly less harmful role.

Sadly, the damage had already been done. The public had no choice but to acclimatise to the air, which was becoming increasingly difficult to breathe. For some, the sudden blast of oxygen that hit them in the face on leaving the city's perimeter was too overwhelming. They much preferred the grimy gas they'd grown used to inhaling.

Since Mercer's reign as Environment Minister, no form of vegetation other than cacti was willing to live in the Dirty City. If an item as innocent as a bunch of flowers entered the city's outer circle, they'd immediately wither and die.

Years later, when Mercer was found dead in his Clean City apartment with the vibrant green murder weapon ditched by his side, the photograph was distributed over the internet with captions such as "Always was a prickly one" and "Try worming your way out of this one, pal."

His killer was never caught.

11

There was a storyteller who lived on Jennifer's 27th floor. Neighbours passed him on the corridor occasionally, and vaguely recognised him from his brief television appearances. No one could be quite sure of his name.

Often when neighbours bumped into the storyteller, he'd invite them in for a cup of coffee. Often a coffee would turn into a brandy.

The neighbours were hugely entertained by his recollections of old-school showbiz. They chimed along with his highly infectious chuckle.

It wasn't until a couple of brandies later that the neighbours grew to realise how meaningless and inconsequential each of his tales were. There was an anecdote about a famous rock star losing his comb. There was another about a football star mistaking a lollypop lady for his mother.

A couple of hours later, part way through a story about a movie actor's goldfish, the neighbours would make their excuses and leave.

It was a shame, they reflected later. The subject matter may have been dull, but the tales were extraordinarily well told. He could've been a great storyteller if he hadn't met all those famous people.

12

The greatest storyteller of all time lived on the 22nd floor. His ability to embellish his extensive life experience astounded anyone he shared it with. Sometimes he'd make stories up on the spot that were better than anything that had ever been printed on paper.

Whenever he ran into a new neighbour, he'd invite them out for a drink. The neighbours spent a fascinating, entertaining and at times highly emotional evening, listening to the storyteller speak.

The neighbours would return to their apartments feeling strangely empty. It took some time to figure it out, but the following morning it would occur to them that the storyteller wasn't their friend. They knew everything about him, and he knew nothing about them. The next time he'd invite them out, they'd make their excuses.

It was a shame, they later reflected. He could've been a great guy if he wasn't a total genius.

13

There was a boy who created one hundred stories a day. Some of them were pretty good.

If anyone had known, they'd've called it a shame. He could've been a great storyteller if only he'd shared.

His name was Lester.

14

There was a rock band called The Susan Killers. The lead singer's name was Defo Tresor.

Very little was known about Defo because he'd never been interviewed. No one knew what he looked like, or even how old he was.

When the band performed live, he delivered his vocals while encased in a wooden crate. In photo-shoots, the less-reclusive guitarist, bassist and drummer were pictured with the crate alongside them. As their fame and notoriety grew, the image of Defo's unconventional stage outfit became an unlikely rock icon.

After its basic chipboard frame appeared on the cover of a leading music magazine, the band ceremoniously burned the crate live on stage, while Defo watched through the peephole of a cardboard box.

From that point on, Defo performed from the inside of a different container every night. One night he performed an entire gig from the confines of a filing cabinet. Another night, an upturned skip. For some concerts, the entire band performed within a storage locker.

It went without saying that no one knew where Defo Tresor lived. Considering the amount of money he made, fans would've been surprised (although not exactly shocked) to discover Defo lived in one of Jennifer's smaller apartments. For some reason, his neighbours had failed to detect him either, despite the fact that the band regularly rehearsed in his living room, usually at a highly anti-social volume.

As their fame escalated, Defo grew more and more paranoid that his face would end up being outed. He wondered if it were possible to erase every single photograph he'd ever appeared in. He'd already persuaded his family (after much pleading and a certain amount of bribery) to delete every photo they'd ever taken of him, but there were plenty of shots still in existence. There were pictures from his college days before he became a recluse, most of which his friends had agreed to dispose of. He was confident he'd eventually manage to track every single one of these down.

More problematically, he'd appeared in various wedding photos, including one where he'd been the best man. It took some negotiating to persuade the bride and groom to airbrush his face out.

Even after that, Defo wasn't happy. He knew there were many more pictures bearing his image that he didn't even know about.

After researching his options, Defo heard a story about a woman living on Jennifer's 10th floor. Her name was Hetty.

Not expecting a great deal, Defo made an appointment.

"Hello," he said as Hetty opened the door.

"Defo Tresor!" she greeted.

Instinctively, Defo covered his face and peeped through his fingers. "I didn't tell you my name," he said. "How did you know...?"

"Your voice, of course. Unmistakable."

Hetty proceeded to deliver an interesting rendition of one of Defo's songs. Defo stood in polite silence.

"Sorry," she said. "I'm a big fan."

Realising Defo was still speechless, she added, "Don't worry – your secret's safe with me."

"Thanks," he said. "I appreciate it."

"So, what can I do for you?"

"Well, I'm trying to track down every single photograph that's ever been taken of me. I'm hoping you'll be able to help."

"Sure," said Hetty.

She led him into the apartment, through the kitchen and into a darkened corner. She directed him towards a door marked "Archived Lives." This happened to be the title of The Susan Killers' second album.

"You named the room after our record?" said Defo.

"I'd like to say yes," said Hetty, "but I thought of it way before you did."

"Oh right."

"Out of interest," she said, "how did you come up with the name Archived Lives?"

"Well, I quite like the idea of walking into a room in which the details of your life are documented in the finest detail, and stored for posterity. It's a metaphor for something, I think."

"Funny you should say that," said Hetty.

"Why?"

She gestured towards the door. "Go ahead."

Defo gently pushed the door open to reveal a small room containing several six-foot stacks of old-fashioned photo albums.

For a moment or so, Defo was unsure as to whether he was willing to open one. Giving into his curiosity, he grabbed an album, opening a page at random.

Inside was a picture of a man and woman standing at the gateway to a flashy building in the Clean City known as The Strawberry. They were smiling. Defo guessed correctly that the couple were tourists.

"Who are these people?" he said.

"The question is," said Hetty, "who's that standing behind them?"

Defo looked twice, then a third time. Slowly, it dawned on him that he was staring at the back of his own head.

"Where did you get this?" he said.

Hetty shrugged. "You wanted every single picture that's ever been taken of you," she said. "Here they are."

"But how does it work? Where did you get them?"

"Dunno," she said. "The room's different for everyone. Whoever walks in sees a different set of pictures." She peered through the door at the stack of photo albums, looking them up and down with a curious distaste. "I've never really been one for photographs," she said. "I haven't even bothered looking at half of mine. Boring, really." She turned towards the door. "Fancy a cup of tea?"

"I'm fine thanks," said Defo.

"I'll leave you to it then," said Hetty.

Defo turned a page. A school photo. Four hundred and fifty kids standing in a field. Erasing this one from the planet would be an embarrassing task. Contacting his old classmates one by one and politely requesting that they recycle their old memories seemed too much of an extreme measure. There must've been at least five hundred copies of this picture printed, and most of them would still be lurking in dusty drawers. Harmless enough, but that wasn't the point.

He turned the page again. Another tourist shot. As he flicked his way through, it appeared that most of the pictures had been taken unintentionally by strangers. Some contained just a hand or a shoulder. Some tourists had managed to capture Defo and his ex-girlfriend kissing. Bizarrely, in the background of one picture, Defo was halfway through a cartwheel. He had no memory of ever having performed a cartwheel in his life, but the evidence was there.

As he dug deeper, Defo discovered more pictures of himself and his ex-girlfriend. They were taken through a crack in his curtains. For some reason, Defo found this extremely amusing.

Hetty returned to find him sitting cross-legged on the floor, chuckling.

"Everything OK?" she said.

Defo was laughing too hard to respond.

"It's a common reaction," she said.

"Certainly gives you a sense of your own insignificance," he said. "So many millions of people out there – most of them have probably got thousands more photographs of themselves than I do. Billions and billions of images. Why am I so intent on tracking mine down and destroying them? Even the dodgy through-the-curtain shots can remain as far as I'm concerned." Tears rolled down his chuckling cheeks.

"It's OK," said Hetty.

"I'm curious," said Defo, wiping his face on his shirt. "You didn't tell me how this thing works."

"Nothing to do with me," said Hetty. "I should've warned you, really. This place can bring both joy and devastation. Some people are driven to murder or suicide. I don't think the room means any harm – it's just trying to be kind."

"So, you're saying the room's *alive?*" said Defo.

"Everything's alive," said Hetty.

Defo stared at the wall as he digested this statement.

"Oh right," he said.

15

A short time later, for whatever reason, Defo Tresor disappeared. It had been almost twelve years since The Susan Killers formed.

Very few people had seen him in the first place, but those who knew him didn't have a clue as to his whereabouts. His family were keen to create some "Missing" posters, but first they'd need a photograph. No one could track one down. Even his bandmates had sworn never to take his picture.

Nonetheless, a number of fans claimed to have spotted him in various unlikely locations. When asked how they knew it was Defo, they'd reply that the face they'd seen corresponded exactly with the picture in their mind that emerged when listening to his music. Interestingly, the man these people had spotted wasn't actually Defo, but could've easily been his twin.

There are a couple of pervasive stories about what really happened to Defo. The first is that he'd lost all of his money in foolish investments. When the economy collapsed, his fortune went with it.

The next thing to disappear was Defo's creativity. He woke up one morning knowing that he'd never write another song. He was destined to recoup his losses by touring The Susan Killers' greatest hits, his popularity waning year on year. He couldn't bear the thought. But what else could he do?

He read a blog post about the rise of musical tribute acts. It was claimed that in many cases, the impersonators made more money than the artists themselves.

Defo would've been happy to perform every single night. Playing a gig while trapped inside a box felt almost like a rehearsal, but the rabble of voices wailing out his carefully-crafted words was like nothing else on earth.

Defo placed an online request for bandmates. He conducted the auditions from the inside of a wardrobe.

"Don't I get to meet you face to face?" a potential bassist enquired.

"Authenticity is the key to our success," replied Defo's voice. "This is serious, serious, serious business."

It wasn't long before Defo's tribute act, The Kusan Sillers played their first set in the back room of a bar. Defo crouched inside a locked wheelie bin.

Word of mouth began to spread, even before they'd finished their opening song. Fans flocked in from the street. When they ran out of floor space, newcomers listened in through the windows. No one had heard a vocalist imitate Defo so accurately. Many people considered this new vocalist (who named himself Tefo Dresor) to be superior to the man he was impersonating.

As Defo had half-hoped and half-dreaded, The Kusan Sillers became a worldwide success. They even released an album recreating The Susan Killers' *Archived Lives* album note-for-note. The album sold more copies than the original.

After seven successful years, Defo felt it was time to retire. The band's farewell concert took place in a specially-cleared area of the concrete wasteland surrounding his former home. Defo performed from inside a coffin.

It was rumoured that he chose to spend his life inside that very same coffin, having food and drink passed to him through a hatch. Even the staff he'd hired to cook for him weren't allowed to see his face.

Or maybe that was someone else.

16

There was another fable about the fate of Defo Tresor, often exchanged by die-hard fans as a means of easing their heartbreak over their idol's disappearance.

Defo had become famous at an early age. He'd never had a job other than as a musician. His college friends all went off to university and worked part time – mainly as bar and waiting staff. A part of Defo envied them immensely.

He was particularly attracted to the idea of being a waiter. As far as Defo was concerned, waiters were as highly-skilled as musicians. Musicians memorised songs; waiters memorised menus. Both had the challenge of connecting with an often hostile audience.

More than anything, it was the anonymity of waiters that really attracted him. In his view, a good waiter should be entirely forgettable – almost invisible.

The day after he officially disappeared, Defo booked an appointment with a careers adviser.

The adviser asked him what experience he had. He said he'd been in a band.

"What kind of band?" said the adviser.

"Can't tell you," said Defo, "but just so you know, I was in the same job for twelve years."

"Excellent. Staying power is an attractive quality. Have you worked in any other field besides music?"

"Nope," said Defo.

"So, are you hoping to continue your career in the music industry?"

"I want to be a waiter," said Defo.

The adviser examined Defo's expression carefully. "Well," he said slowly. "Let's see what's available."

"You don't look too hopeful," said Defo.

"The only drawback is your lack of experience," said the adviser. "Most restaurant managers want a person who knows how to do the job."

"I could do the job better than half the waiters in the business," Defo snapped. "You see so many of these clowns just going through the motions – no enthusiasm, no passion. In it for the money. I don't care about all that. I just want to get out there and *do* it, man."

"Just one tip," said the adviser. "Don't say that in the interview."

Defo took in a deep breath and exhaled painfully. "So, what shall I say?" he said.

"Let's take a look at the vacancies first, shall we?" The adviser rattled through a series of mouse-clicks. "Just taking a quick ... OK. "Experience essential." Let's try the next one..." – *click* – "Experience essential again. OK..." – *click* – "...Experience essential..." – *click* – "...Experience essential..." – *click* – "...Experience essential..." – *click* – "...and that's it. I'm sorry, Mr Dresor."

"What are you saying?"

"That's all the vacancies for now. You can keep checking online."

"Are they all going to say "Experience essential"?"

"Pretty much."

#

For several days, Defo wandered the streets of the Dirty City looking for restaurants with signs in the window saying "Staff Required".

In a bar, he was treated to a drink by the manager, who declined his request for an interview, but felt moved to offer some advice.

"This isn't what you want to hear," said the manager kindly, "but look around you – people are fleeing the city in search of a better life. Buildings are standing derelict. Restaurants are closing on an hourly basis. Every youngster in the city wants to be a waiter, but the fact of the matter is, there just isn't enough space."

"I'm not giving up," said Defo.

"I admire your spirit."

"Give me a job then."

"Experience essential, I'm afraid."

"Oh."

#

Eventually Defo landed an interview at one of the more upmarket fast-food chains.

Sitting among the queue of candidates was Billy D, his former lead guitarist – one of the few people in the city who'd recognise his face.

"Hey," say Defo, sitting down beside him.

"Defo!" he blurted.

"Shhhh," said Defo softly. "My name's *Tefo*, OK?"

"Sorry," said Billy. "Should've known. It's good to see you."

"Same to you, man," said Defo. "What are you doing here? You had that new band – Potato Heads, is it?"

"Potato Head, actually – singular."

"What happened?"

"I quit – same as you. Music's a dead end. I need to follow my heart. Do what I should've done years ago."

Defo glanced back and forth at the cluster of smart-casual hopefuls waiting for their five-minute conversation with the shift supervisor.

"You know what's sad?" he said. "I've always fantasised about this. I used to practice in front of the mirror with a Frisbee instead of a tray. "Sir? Madam? Sir? Madam?""

"It's not sad," said Billy.

Defo got to his feet. "You know what?" he said. "We need to stop dreaming. How'd you feel about joining me?"

"Joining you where?" said Billy.

"Let's form a band."

"Really?"

"Why not?"

"I can't face it, Defo. The idea of banging out the same chords night after night, rattling through the same old riffs ... If I have to hear you shout "Let me hear you make some noise" one more time..."

"Yeah, I always hated that one."

"So, why do you want to go back?"

Defo shrugged. "Maybe it's all we're good for."

"Suppose so."

"Shall we get out of here?"

"Alright."

They stepped into the car park, breathing in a new kind of air.

"Shall we go for a drink?" said Defo. "Call it a celebration?"

"Sure," said Billy. "Later on, though, yeah? I've got to buy my guitar back from the pawn shop."

"I'll come with you, actually," said Defo.

"Why?" said Billy.

Defo's eyes meandered for a while as he contemplated the statement that followed.

"I need to buy back my box."

17

There was a short period in recent history in which the Dirty City's inhabitants developed the ability to read each other's thoughts.

Citizens awoke one morning to find they could examine the intricate workings of their loved ones' minds, ploughing the depths of their memories for moments of wonder and incriminating archived material. They grew to fully appreciate the beauty and complexity of the human mind. It magnified hatred, love and indifference.

For some, it was a welcome return to an imagined past in which everyone was obliged to engage with their communities. For many, this proved an extremely daunting prospect.

Jennifer's hundred storeys were divided into several small apartments. The extent of the psychic traffic whispering through her walls caused many of her occupants to permanently evacuate. Even after they were gone, the overwhelming barrage of information was almost impossible to bear.

For some, their new-found ability had a positive impact on their mental wellbeing. Relationships blossomed. Lives were enriched by a new form of openness and honesty.

Meanwhile, the murder rate increased rapidly. Anyone with a dark past ran the risk of being immediately killed following the revelation of their unspeakable secrets.

One evening, a man on Jennifer's 23rd floor stuffed a substantial selection of belongings into an undersized suitcase. Before he left, he felt it was only polite to mention the circumstances of his departure to his girlfriend.

"I'm moving out," he stated, flatly. "I won't give a reason out loud."

From force of habit, his girlfriend's mouth popped open in defensive incomprehension.

"Surely you're not denying it?" he said.

"Hang on a minute," she said. "That was a *secret*. You had no right digging around inside my head. If anyone's in the wrong here, it's *you*."

"Me?"

"Yes."

The man dropped his suitcase. It sprang open, spraying socks around the room. "First of all," he said, "I wasn't "digging around." It was right there, *screaming* at me."

"You should've done the decent thing and ignored it," said his girlfriend.

"How am I supposed to do that?"

"It's just not *fair*, that's all. I've always been reassured by the idea that my thoughts are the one thing that can't be stolen. I'm within my rights to harbour as many depraved secrets as I like."

The man stamped his suitcase shut and hauled it towards the door. "That's where you and I differ," he said.

His girlfriend had never been the pleading type. She spoke in a voice neither of them had heard before. "*Please.* Let's not be like those morons upstairs – killing each other all because of some misplaced brainwave energy. Let's just see what's on TV."

"You mean just *forget* about it?"

"I'm saying let's *ignore* it. I've been blocking that particular memory out for *years*. There's no reason why we can't ignore it together."

"No one can ignore anything anymore," he said.

She sighed, and sat down on the couch. "You're right. I never realised how important denial was until it vanished."

"You'll be fine," he said. "You're on your own now. No need to worry about anyone else finding out. No one else'll have you."

He opened the door.

"I know what you did too," she said.

The man stood motionless. He didn't say anything, and didn't need to.

He turned to face her. He dropped his case on the floor and sat down beside her.

"What's on TV then?" he said.

18

During that time, there were many political scandals. For a brief while, after several corrupt MPs had been booted out of office, the public's newfound skill of mindreading was seen as ushering in the era of the honest politician. The first to take full advantage was former Environment Minister, Jeremy Mercer.

Whenever Mercer appeared in public, a new scandal broke. He'd awarded himself a range of bogus qualifications; he'd fabricated evidence that led to a range of rivals being removed from office; he'd brokered secret arms deals that had made him millions in illicit payments.

Eventually, Mercer made a public statement:

"Yes," he said, "I never actually finished college. Yes, I've orchestrated the career suicide of anyone that stood in my way. Yes, I've bent over backwards for an orderly queue of industries, accidentally becoming a multi-millionaire in the process. So what? Doesn't the fact that I've been so successful in continuously conning the public make me a highly intelligent man? Who better to run the city's affairs? Would you really prefer a smiling simpleton in a suit?

"There's a reason crooked politicians exist, my friends. As despicable as we are, we're preferable to the alternative. The last thing anyone wants is a yes man.

"Sure, I've lied. I'm glad I was found out. I'm glad everyone knows everything about everyone. Who better to lead this new age than a man who's spent his entire career lying through his teeth?"

Following Mercer's speech, several members of the audience were admitted to hospital having broken their fingers from clapping too enthusiastically.

19

During the same period, there was a living myth known as the Slumber Fairy. Her real name was Eliza.

As tormentors go, Eliza was relatively benign. She may have broken into a multitude of homes on a nightly basis, but she never stole anything physical.

All but the most isolated inhabitants of the Dirty City had already had the pleasure or the horror of tapping into a loved one's head while they were sleeping. Some deliberately stayed awake to see what delights their housemates had in store.

At that time, Eliza was working night shifts in a home for the elderly. A late-night tour of the residents' bedrooms was like channel-surfing across infinity – brainfuls of experience and repressed imagination, intensified by a barrage of psychotropic pharmaceuticals.

One thing she grew to appreciate was that each person's dreams are unique – sometimes subtly, often wildly. If dreams are movies, each of them have a different writer, director and cast.

Eliza wanted to be the world's first dream-buff. She'd never be able to get through them all, but she could make a fair attempt at capturing the psychological makeup of each resident of the Dirty City.

Although she never entirely fulfilled this ambition, she was an incredibly successful burglar. She left no fingerprints. Her crimes were committed all over the city, seemingly at random, which meant there was no indication of where she lived. Indeed, there was no firm proof that Eliza's break-ins were committed by the same person.

If you happened to possess an exceptionally creative subconscious, it was likely you'd be broken into on a regular basis. Unimaginative types were ignored completely. This was the only pattern the authorities were able to identify.

When it became apparent that the Slumber Fairy was more likely to target artists, writers and musicians, a break-in became a badge of honour among certain sections of the creative community. There were several proven cases of artists falsely claiming to have fallen victim to the Slumber Fairy in a desperate attempt to appear interesting.

All sorts of rumours and superstitions emerged. It was claimed that not only did the Slumber Fairy read your mind, she also removed the dream completely. Whenever you woke up having not remembered a single one of your dreams, it was because the Slumber Fairy had stolen them.

#

One evening, in her search for new minds to unlock, Eliza encountered a boy living on Jennifer's 47th floor.

His door was unlocked. She crept inside to find him sitting on the floor.

"I'm so sorry!" she exclaimed.

"It's OK," said Lester.

"Honestly, this is the first time I've walked in on someone awake. I don't know how that happened."

"Pleased to meet you anyway," said Lester, dipping into her mind for a moment. "Eliza, right?"

"I thought you'd be more surprised," she said.

"Why?"

"Because you've probably been wondering what the Slumber Fairy looks like."

"What's a Slumber Fairy?" said Lester.

Eliza couldn't help feeling a slight pin-prick to her ego.

"You don't get out much, do you?" she said.

"No," he said.

Lester examined her mind a little further. "You know, I'm wondering why you bother breaking into people's houses at all," he said. "You read people's minds through the wall in the first place, checking if they're asleep."

"I like the intensity of being up close."

"I see what's happened, by the way," said Lester. "I was making up a story, which you mistook for a dream."

"Makes sense," she said.

"You know what I like about dreams?" said Lester. "It's the way they end right in the middle. It's a cliff hanger without a sequel. You'll never know what was supposed to happen in the end, even though it was your own mind that wrote the script."

"Tell me the story," said Eliza. "The one you were just creating."

"Give me a minute," he said.

20

There was a man who had one of those dreams about having a dream. Within that dream, he dreamt of having another dream – and so it went on. Pretty soon, the man lost count of the number of rabbit holes he'd snuck his way into.

When he finally awoke, he couldn't be sure if he were dreaming or not. He had no choice but to live his life as though nothing was real. His actions no longer had consequences. He could open his eyes at any moment.

Nothing much changed. He didn't quit work, sell his apartment, murder his noisy neighbours and then go backpacking. He persevered with his dismal job. As much as he disliked the rock band who rehearsed nightly above him, he remained in his apartment, listening to their relentless droning bass-wibbles until the early hours of the morning. These irritations didn't affect him anymore. They didn't exist.

One afternoon, he crossed the street without looking and was hit by an ambulance.

When his eyes slammed shut, it didn't feel like death. It felt like he was finally waking up.

#

"That's an ending," said Lester.

21

"So, what about your own dreams?" said Eliza. "Do you have a favourite?"

"I haven't really thought about it," said Lester. "I tend not to categorise these things."

"Fair enough," said Eliza.

"I had a dream the other day where there weren't any right angles. All the buildings in the city were leaning towers. Their windows were isosceles triangles. The cars on the road were spherical – rolling metal boulders with circular windows.

"No one stood up straight. Tourists in the street looked like branches sprouting diagonally from the pavement. You couldn't bend your elbows or your knees past a certain point. It was restrictive, but somehow it was more liberating than the world I was used to.

"It was one of those dreams where you know you're dreaming. I didn't want to wake up. I wanted to live in the Diagonal City, with its endless curves and spikes."

Eliza nodded along thoughtfully.

"That's it, really," he said. "That's the thing with dreams – there's no plot. Like I say, I kind of like the idea of there not being an ending. But sometimes you need a conclusion. You need someone to tap you on the shoulder and explain what it all means."

"Maybe it doesn't mean anything," said Eliza.

"Everything means something," said Lester.

"What do you mean?"

Lester thought about it for a while.

"I don't know," he said.

22

"Do *you* have a favourite dream?" he said. "You've experienced more than most."

"The trouble is," said Eliza, "it's the nightmares that stick. You forget your happy dreams in a flash, but terrible ones can haunt you for weeks. In some cases, they'll drive you out of your mind."

"I know," he said. "Irritating, isn't it?"

"I'll tell you about the worst dream I ever witnessed," said Eliza. "I know you've never heard of me, but it's been well-documented that I visit the homes of prominent creative types. Some of them deliberately leave their doors open in a bid to entice me. Boosts their reputation, apparently. In the case of this particular artist, great lengths had been taken to ensure no one ever broke in. There were fortified combination locks, a sophisticated alarm system and four pitbull terriers. Clearly the guy had something to hide."

"So, how did you get in?"

She shrugged. "It's easy enough to disable alarms when you've had the practise. All you need to do to open combination locks is read the person's mind. As for the dogs, they were asleep. Have you ever read a pitbull's dreams?"

"No."

"They're not that interesting. Anyway, as soon as I was inside the house, the artist's subconscious screamed out at me. I didn't dare step any further. If I'd've stepped into his bedroom, I'm not sure my head could've coped with the sheer force."

"What happened?"

"It was the worst kind of nightmare," she said. "Recurring. When I say recurring, I mean the guy had experienced the same dream every single night since the age of fourteen."

"How old was he?"

"Fifty-six. That's a lot of nightmares."

"So, what happened?"

Eliza closed her eyes, trying to find the appropriate words. "The artist dreamt he was being swallowed up by colour. He'd open his eyes and all he could see was green, or red, or whatever. It was a different colour every night. He felt his body slowly corroding under the impact. He couldn't move. He couldn't open his mouth. He couldn't breathe or feel his heartbeat. All he could hear or feel was PURPLE! PURPLE! PURPLE!"

Lester flinched as his companion shouted in his face – "PURPLE! PURPLE!"

"OK," said Lester, waving her away. "I get the point."

"But do you *really* get the point?" said Eliza. "Imagine being screamed at by colours every single night. Can you picture it?"

"Don't think so," said Lester.

Eliza sat back, breathlessly. "Incidentally," she said, "the artist spent his entire career working in charcoal. I don't know if that's relevant. I don't know what any of it means."

"Everything means something," said Lester.

"Stop saying that," she said. "You know what that little statement of yours is?"

"Go on."

"It's meaningless. Meaningless."

"OK. Sorry."

23

Then, overnight, the inhabitants of the Dirty City reverted back to their five basic senses.

Eliza paid a visit to Lester's apartment. From force of habit, she strolled in through the unlocked door.

"Well," said Lester, "it's a good job I wasn't naked."

"Sorry," said Eliza. "I'll have to get used to this."

"I suppose that's it, then?" said Lester.

"*It?*"

"You're coming to say farewell?"

"What makes you think that?"

"Because you no longer have access to my thoughts."

"Lester," she said, "you may have forgotten, but I never read your mind in the first place. We shared stories the old-fashioned way."

"So, that's what you're here for?" said Lester. "More stories?"

"I'm not sure why I'm here," she said.

He looked out of the window. "I've got an idea," he said. "Why don't the two of us sit together in silence?"

"You're asking me to shut up?"

"Not in those words."

They sat down together and closed their eyes. They cleared their minds of clutter. They ignored everything, including each other.

Several hours later, Eliza snapped out of her trance. "Thanks Lester," she said.

Lester opened his eyes. "Thank you too," he said.

As Eliza left, she felt her mind filling up once again with the triviality of everyday life. The memory of her afternoon with Lester lingered more than her many nightmares.

24

There was a large hill just outside the Dirty City's perimeter, slightly higher than any of its man-made structures. At the top of the hill was a colossal white building with gleaming thirty-foot high gates. Owing to its upward distance from the city streets, the building was known as Mile Prison.

One day, in an apartment on Jennifer's 88th floor, a little girl and her mother were eating breakfast. For no apparent reason, the girl plonked her spoon into her half-eaten bowl of cereal and rushed across to the window.

"What's that?" she asked her mother.
"It's Mile Prison, darling," said her mother quietly.
"What's a prison?"
"Do we have to talk about this now? You'll be late for school."
"*Tell* me."
"OK. Prison is where they take bad people and lock them away."
"Why do they do that?"
"For our protection, darling. So the bad people can't get us."
"What happens to the bad people once they're in there?"
"Nothing. They sit there and think about what they've done."
"How long for?"
"Forever."
"For-*ever?*"
"I mean for the rest of their lives."

The girl gazed up at the gleaming white gates. The building certainly didn't look like it was intended to house criminals.

"So, is that where they took Daddy?" she said.

Her mother's response was firm and immediate: *"Eat your breakfast."*

"I ought to know where he is."

"Fine. That's where they took him. I'm sorry to say this, darling, but your father isn't coming back. He lives in Mile Prison now. We'll never see him again. *Eat your cereal.*"

The girl returned to her bowl and swirled the milk around with her spoon. "Maybe I could do something bad," she said.

"Don't be stupid."

"If I do something bad, I'll get to see Daddy again."

"Darling."

"Maybe I could rob a bank or kill someone."

"That's *enough*."

"Or I could blow something up."

"So, what would happen to me?" said her mother. "I'd never see you again."

"Oh," said the girl. "I didn't think of that."

"So, you're not going to do anything bad?"

"Sorry Mum."

The girl swirled her spoon some more, spilling a few droplets onto the table top.

"Do you think he can see us from up there?" she said. "We'd just be tiny dots, but he can figure out which apartment window to look through. He just needs to count the floors."

"Maybe," said her mother.

"I like the idea of him watching over us."

"It's a nice idea, darling, but I don't think they put the prison up there so that the prisoners can watch the world below."

"So, what did they put it there for?"

"I believe the prison was built on the hill so that wherever you are in the Dirty City, you're reminded of where you'll end up if you do something bad. It stares you in the face, day and night. Even when the curtains are drawn, you can feel it *watching* you. *"I'll get you,"* it says. *"I'll rip you away from your loved ones. I'll make you wish you'd never been conceived.""*

The apartment suddenly felt very cold.

"Does it really make you feel like that?" said the girl.

"No," said her mother. "Not really. Ignore me. I was being silly. Eat your cereal."

"OK."

The girl picked up her spoon, and slowly forced it between her pursed lips.

25

"So, what sort of things do you do?" said Lester. "I mean, when you're not with me?"

"Why do you want to know?" said Eliza.

"Just curious."

"Looks like you'll have to carry on being curious."

Lester wasn't sure whether he should be bewildered or offended. "Why can't you tell me?" he said.

"I *could* tell you," she said. "I've chosen not to."

"How come?"

"Makes me more interesting. My life's been pretty dull since the Slumber Fairy retired, but I wouldn't want people to know that. Much better to maintain an air of mystery."

Lester grinned. "Nice move," he said. "You're like a story."

"In what way?"

"Fiction's all about the things the storyteller doesn't tell you."

"You reckon?"

"Yeah."

"So what about you?" she said. "Are you like a story?"

"My life's pretty uninteresting too," said Lester. "All I ever do is sit in my apartment making things up. I'm much happier saying things that aren't true. I realise that sounds kind of tragic."

"It's not tragic at all," said Eliza.

"I know," said Lester. "It's *great*."

"Nothing better than being alone," she said. "But for *me*..."

"What?"

"There's something missing."

"Like what?"

"I don't know. I don't want to sound too much like a superhero, but it feels like the city needs me."

"What for?"

"I don't know. *Something*. I need to think about it some more. Tell me a story."

"What about?" said Lester.

"Anything," she said.

"Have I told you about Orange Street Hospital yet?"

"Orange what?"

"OK. Listen."

26

At one time, the maternity ward in Orange Street Hospital was home to a phenomenon called "conjoined consciousness". There were several cases of twins being born with separate bodies but one mind.

Detection of the condition didn't happen overnight, but it wasn't long before the parents' suspicions were aroused. One twin always knew what the other was doing. You could ask one child a question and the other would respond. By the time they were old enough to explain it for themselves, the diagnosis was already clear.

From a conjoined twin's perspective, there were many advantages to having an extra brain and body. You were twice as intelligent. You could literally be in two places at once. Above all else, it was an excellent party trick.

Naturally, there were downsides. Decision-making was a particular issue. In extreme cases, disagreements between siblings could lead to an acute sense of self-loathing.

The phenomenon was by no means restricted to twins. There was one case in which a girl and her mother ended up with a conjoined mind. From day one, the baby herself had access to all of her mother's thoughts and memories. Her first ever thought was: "So, this is what it's like to be born."

Later, she thought: "So, this is what it's like to be breast-fed." / "So, this is what it's like gazing up at my own face." / "So, this is what I sound like to other people." / "So, this is what it's like to be loved by everyone I meet." / "So this is what it's like to have no responsibilities." / "So, this is what it's *like*."

At first, the mother thought she was simply feeling an extreme level of empathy with the child.

Then, gradually, the side of her that was a newborn baby began to think independently. She began to think and feel like a genuine newborn. No knowledge, no memories, no awareness, just sleep, drink, wriggle, cry, sleep, drink, wriggle, cry.

As the child grew up, her mother felt herself getting younger and younger. Her body may have been thirty six, but her mind was being dragged towards infancy. The child herself grew old beyond her years, even as her body remained tiny. Equipped with her mother's memories, she knew everything there was to know about childhood, and couldn't be bothered to live through the whole thing again.

At the age of four, the child announced to the world that she wasn't four at all – she was seventeen.

At the same time, her mother declared that she too was seventeen years old. "It was my happiest year," she explained to her younger self. "I met your father. He taught me how to bake bread. I taught him karate and the meaning of life. It was a wonderful summer."

They made a pact that day. Whatever happened to their bodies from that point on, they'd remain at the age of seventeen, constantly reliving those blissful days in August, nineteen years previously. They cut themselves off from the world, and ended up incredibly happy.

If there was a lesson to be learned, it was that cutting yourself off from the world isn't too much of a bad thing.

27

There were several cases of Orange Street midwives becoming accidentally conjoined with babies they'd been delivering.

Not least of all was the story of Eleanor Longer. The first time Eleanor accidentally attached herself to a baby, she visited the child's family on a regular basis. She was able to articulate all the boy's impulses before he was able to speak.

"I'd like to be winded please," she'd say with a childlike smile. "Then sleep. Lots of it."

"What's it like being a baby?" the parents would ask.

"Difficult to say," said Eleanor. "Sometimes I find myself losing language altogether. I close my eyes, and there's nothing but a jumble of colours. Grey, blue, red, silver. Starfish swirl after starfish swirl. Sometimes it's like I'm floating through a tunnel – like a near-death experience, but instead of a bright light at the end, there's just white. I'm not sure what the white is, exactly. I think it might be milk."

Soon after, during an early morning shift, Eleanor acquired another child. She picked up a third a week later. Pretty soon, it became almost a daily occurrence.

A month or so later, Eleanor shared her mind with no less than seventeen babies. By that point, she decided to do the sensible thing, and leave the hospital.

"There's way, way, way too much going on," she told her seventeen other selves.

She tendered her resignation and moved into an inexpensive apartment on Jennifer's 59th floor.

As her seventeen babies grew, she experienced constant pain and relentless joy. When one was crying another was being tickled.

That, of course, was just the beginning. She went through puberty seventeen times simultaneously. The only way she could deal with the pressure was to lock herself away in her apartment, staring out of the window at the concrete sea, hoping for better days.

Better and worse days arrived. It was difficult to keep track of what each version of her was up to. They all had different genes, different families and cultures. Yet, they were so close together – all within the northern section of the city.

It was the closeness that really tested their collective sanity. Every time a couple of them bumped into each other in the street, there was a sickening sense of magnetism, as though their brains were being sucked into one another.

One by one, each of Ms Longer's component parts departed to various far flung destinations.

Eventually, only Eleanor remained, sitting in her apartment, staring out at the concrete with a fixed smile, and the trace of a tear in her swirly, swirly eye.

28

There was a boy named Zane who was born with the mind of his billionaire father, who'd died shortly before he was born at the age of thirty.

This wasn't reincarnation. Throughout his lifetime, Zane's father (also called Zane) claimed to be simultaneously living the life of his own son, thirty years in the future. Consequently, he was able to accurately predict technological advancements, and major world events. He made his billions through a series of investments based on his observations of the future stock market.

The two Zanes hated each other. They were more like rival siblings than father and son. When Zane's mother compared notes with his grandmother, they came to the same conclusion: the boys were frustrated that they were unable to fight it out in person. A playful scrap would've rid them of any minor animosity. Instead, their dislike for each other intensified as each year passed.

As soon as he was old enough, Zane Junior donated his eight-figure inheritance to charity. He sold his house in the Clean City, and moved into an apartment on Jennifer's least expensive floor (which happened to be the 78th).

He hated his father for his unpunishable acts of fraud. His father hated him for giving his billions away out of sheer spite.

In the end, it was Zane Junior who had the upper hand. He'd heard the story of how Zane Senior had died, but for whatever reason, he'd always chosen to keep this knowledge locked away in the furthest corner of his mind. His father never knew nor suspected.

Occasionally, one half of their unfortunate partnership was able to influence the actions of the other. They may not have been able to fight it out, but sometimes Zane Senior was able to summon up enough psychic energy to make Zane Junior slap himself across the face. One time, Zane Junior took it upon himself to cause his father to dive head first into a frozen lake.

On reaching the age of thirty, Zane Junior knew his father wasn't going to live to see thirty-one. He knew exactly when and how it would happen. He knew he'd feel his pain. He'd know what it's like to die, and would remember it until his own passing.

When his father climbed into his jeep and set off speeding through the city, it occurred to Zane that if he wanted to, he could influence his father's behaviour. He could change history and keep him alive.

Instead, in a snap, Zane ever-so-subtly nudged his father's hand at the wheel.

As the car burst into flames, Zane collected many new experiences in the space of a second. He didn't just know what it was like to die. He knew what it was like to lose 50% of your mind; he knew what it was like to kill; he knew what it was like to be guilty of a crime for which he'd never be convicted.

As he negotiated his way through his thirties, Zane gained another new experience: he knew what it was like to keep hold of a secret that no one else would ever know. He even managed to hide it from himself a fair amount of the time.

Inevitably perhaps, it became impossible for Zane's secret to remain within his skull's solitary cell.

In his years living in Jennifer, he'd often wondered what the roof looked like. He'd always assumed that access was restricted to maintenance staff. One night, out of curiosity, he pressed the button in the lift and was surprised to find himself deposited into the open air.

It was too dark for him to see where he was creeping. No stars, no moon. The city lights below were a distant haze.

Zane stumbled across the concrete.

He raised his arms to the sky.

"I know you can't hear me," he said to the air, "but I needed to tell someone."

His confession began with his birth. He needed to recount the whole story in order for it to make sense. By the time he'd finished, it was three and a half hours later. All that time caged up in his head had allowed the story to develop into a full-blown epic.

"It's OK," said a voice.

The words hit him like a bullet to the chest. He just about managed to prevent himself falling flat on his back.

He looked to his left to see a boy's face half-visible through candlelight.

"Who are you?" he said.

"My name's Lester," said the boy. "Sorry to startle you. I couldn't help overhearing."

"I'm rehearsing," said Zane quickly. "A play. A one-man show."

"Really?" said Lester.

Zane's eyes darted around for a while, suddenly conscious that Lester may not have been the only eavesdropper. "I'm sorry," he said. "You're not going to tell anyone, are you?"

"I don't have anyone to tell," said Lester.

"It's not really a confession anyway," said Zane. "I'm just trying to make sense of it all. I've never been able to figure out what happened in those few seconds. I never intended to kill him."

"So, why did you do it?" said Lester.

"I didn't want to meet him," said Zane. "I couldn't imagine a life with that man as my father. There's no power like a father's hold over his son. Or so they tell me."

"But you *were* him," said Lester.

"Not me," said Zane. "A part of me. The part of me I've always been appalled by. As I say, this isn't a confession of guilt. I'm glad I killed him, and I'd do it again. I just don't understand what any of this means."

He paused, almost expecting Lester to offer an explanation. Lester blinked back at him.

"I should see a shrink, really," said Zane. "I'm a psychoanalyst's fantasy patient. Always had a funny relationship with my mother."

"Do you feel better now?" said Lester.

Zane shivered as though he'd only just realised it was cold. "I do, actually," he said. "It's good to get these things out in the open, so to speak. What are you doing here anyway?"

"Listening," said Lester. "It's surprising how many people come up here to declare their darkest secrets to the stars."

"So, what do you do? Just sit here waiting for tortured souls like me to turn up?"

"It's kind of like fishing," said Lester.

"Seems wrong."

"I think of it as a valued service," said Lester. "I'm not here to judge anyone. I'm just here to listen."

"Sounds great, actually," said Zane. "Mind if I join you sometime?"

"Actually," said Lester, "if it's all the same, this is more of a solitary pursuit."

"I understand," said Zane. "Just an idea."

29

Over the months that followed, Lester continued to nestle himself discreetly on Jennifer's roof, waiting patiently for his neighbours to creep up and declare their secrets.

One resident was a regular confessor. He began his first visit by declaring:

"Greetings, No one! I'd rather not give my name. You can call me The Observer, if you like. My brain's so full of confidential information, it's time for at least some of it to be released back into the ether.

"I don't just keep my own secrets, you see. I *watch* people. It's a strange relationship, really. They don't know me, yet I know things about them that even their closest friends don't. Have I done anything wrong, I wonder? I protect other people's private lives just as carefully as I protect my own. I just need to *tell* someone, even if it's No one.

"Having said that, you're not strictly No one, are you? I'm assuming there's at least one Peeping Tom on this roof. Maybe you're the same Peeping Tom who's planted a camera in my bathroom. If you are, I'm sure you'll never share the secrets I'm about to impart, just as you'll never share the footage of me showering.

"I have many stories to tell, but I might as well begin with the celebrities. I'm name-dropping as much as anything else. I spent six months stalking Defo Tresor from The Susan Killers, for example. I could tell you what he looks like if you wanted to know. I could tell you that he spent the majority of his music career living under this very roof, undetected by anyone other than myself. I can confirm that he isn't dead. He may have disappeared without a trace, but I still know where he lives.

"For a while, Defo lived in a relatively modest house on the outskirts of the Clean City. During that time, I spent at least eight hours a day hiding in the postbox across the street. Collection times weren't exactly like clockwork, but they were reliable enough for me to enter and exit undetected. I'd pop out for half an hour's coffee break before skeleton-keying my way back in.

"On busy days, it could get pretty cramped, but on the plus side, there was plenty to read. That's right, fellow stalker, I must confess to opening other people's mail. Can't get enough of it. Say what you like, but I've never actually stolen anything. Even if the envelopes contained enormous wads of cash, I'd still seal them back up.

"I sifted my way through all sorts – love letters, death threats, suicide notes, the works. There are many stories I could share, but let's stick with my own for now.

"The slot allowed me a more than adequate view of Defo's living room, and the bedroom above. He had a habit of leaving the curtains half-open, for which I'm eternally grateful. The resulting photographs are among my most prized possessions.

"When Defo's mysterious female companion arrived on the scene, I suppose you could say things were getting interesting. Not for me, I'm afraid. I'd been attracted to Defo because I felt I could relate to his songs in a way no one else could. If you're familiar with The Susan Killers, and have bothered to listen to the lyrics, you'll know Mr Tresor writes almost exclusively about isolation. Unlike many of his whining contemporaries, Defo doesn't sing about loneliness. He sings about the joys of solitude and seperateness. Aside from yourself, it's been some time since I actually spoke to a real person. Believe it or not, I prefer things this way.

"It all changed when he found himself a girlfriend. Defo was no longer the silent genius he once was. He'd *blended in*.

"The final photograph I took was of the two of them kissing. I've got nothing against people enjoying themselves, but somehow I found it an utterly repulsive sight.

"I wasn't actually disappointed. I was relieved to have a neat little ending to my unhealthy obsession. I was happy I didn't have to sit in a postbox for eight hours a day anymore.

"I still kept my eye on Defo from time to time. The story of what happened between him and his ex-girlfriend is an interesting one. I'll share that tomorrow.

"Night night."

30

The following evening, The Observer stepped onto the roof and said: "As I was saying ..."

Lester shuffled a little closer.

"When I began stalking Defo Tresor, I was something of an amateur. I was yet to begin installing hidden recording devices in people's living rooms, or squatting in their attics with my ear to the floor. I may have lost interest in Defo, but by some pure fluke, he moved back to Jennifer, a couple of floors up from my place. By this point I was a far more accomplished spy. Seen as he was a couple of flights of stairs away, I thought I might as well break in while he was out. I installed a camera in an unused wall socket, and kept him under observation.

"One thing I've learned is that Defo talks to himself a lot. He's a mumbler, so I had to crank up the volume pretty high.

"One morning he stood in the bathroom, shaving expertly with the edge of a broken beer bottle. Eye-to-eye with his reflection, he mumbled: "Why are you with her in the first place, Defo? Why am I even asking that question? You're with her because you wanted to fall in love. You wanted to fall in love because you wanted to write love songs. You've written a few – that'll do, eh? Don't want to labour the point. Only one thing for it now – you'll have to break up. Sacrifice your happiness so you can write about heartbreak. Go on – you know you want to."

"Sure enough, that afternoon, Defo ended their relationship with a brief, tearful phone call. He stayed in his apartment for six weeks, during which time he completed the ten songs that would make up The Susan Killers' third album, *It's All Abstract*.

"I don't know if you're familiar with *It's All Abstract*, Dear Listener, but you can be forgiven for not realising it contains possibly the most beautiful, devastating love songs known to humankind. The album consists of thundering drums, bass, guitars and the occasional triangle, with Defo whispering softly beneath. There aren't any lyrics in the sleeve notes. Even if you pick apart the audio, Defo's voice is slurred and distorted. Fans would've had the opportunity to lipread were it not for the fact that Defo only ever performed inside a box.

"As far as I'm aware, the only two people in the world who know the words to the greatest love songs of all time are myself and Defo. Apologies for not sharing them with you, my fellow voyeur. There are some secrets that I'll take to my grave."

31

"Another name-drop for you," said The Observer. "Jeremy Mercer. He's been called an incompetent politician, and as it happens, he's equally incompetent when it comes to home security. I was able to walk into his unlocked apartment any time I liked. Whenever he caught me, I told him I'd come to repair the light fittings. He was more than happy to accept my claim. One time he caught me hiding in his wardrobe. I told him I was looking for a flat-head screwdriver. He said, "No problem – they're in the bottom drawer – help yourself to whatever you need."

"In the drawer there was a padded envelope containing a hundred thousand dollars. Having tapped Mercer's phone, I was fully aware that he'd been offered the cash by a large insurance company in exchange for turning a blind eye to their substantial tax evasion.

"I placed the money back in the envelope, pulled out a flat-head screwdriver and returned to the wardrobe.

"Later that day, Mercer made a phone call to a children's charity, donating ninety-five thousand dollars. He then made a phone call to his press officer. His plan was to take the story to the newspapers, blowing the whistle on the firm who'd paid him off, while sparking off an ethical debate over the prospect of accepting a bribe in order to save children's lives (and whether or not five grand was an acceptable finder's fee).

"If you're wondering why you never heard the story, it turns out the insurance company bribed the press to remain silent. To Mercer's extreme annoyance, the version of the story that appeared in the papers was: "Jeremy Mercer donates ninety-five thousand dollars to a children's charity."

"To his credit, Mercer has made it clear in public that his image is far more important to him than his policies. The last thing he wanted was to be portrayed as a goody two shoes.

"The morning the story broke, he had a lengthy conversation with his lawyer. That afternoon, he made a public statement saying: "I would like it on record that I *absolutely did not* donate ninety-five thousand dollars to a children's charity. I hate kids almost as much as I detest charitable causes."

"There was a short round of applause."

32

"In the corner of Mercer's office there was a large paper shredder. The bin was large enough to squat in, and the paper slot was just about wide enough for me to peep through. One day, Mercer entered the office, opened his safe, and pulled out a mountain of paperwork.

"He sat at the desk, strenuously studying. Every ten minutes or so, after reading through one of the documents, he'd feed it through the shredder into my hair. As the afternoon wore on, the paper formed a nest around my middle. As the nest grew larger and denser, I was beginning to develop serious fears of suffocation.

"*Typical*, I thought. *Dying while prying into a politician's secrets after hours of failing to learn anything even vaguely interesting*.

"My mind was put at rest after I'd calculated the size of the remaining stack. By my reckoning, Mercer had enough paper to bury me up to the neck, leaving me with minimal breathing space but not quite threatening my life.

"By the time Mercer had reached his final document, I'd struck upon a strategy. As he posted the paperwork through, I managed to claw one of my hands free, grabbing hold of a page of stick-thin strips.

"I made my escape once the coast was clear, taking the handful of shreds back to my apartment. I spent the remainder of the evening arranging them back into a legible sheet of A4.

"What I discovered was appallingly exciting. Mercer had compiled a document detailing the personal details of a randomly-selected member of the public, including family history, bank account information and medical records. Presumably this was one of countless others. Surely I wasn't spying on another Peeping Tom.

"When I returned to Mercer's office the following day, I was pleased to discover he'd emptied the shredder bin. I climbed inside.

"Mercer arrived a short while later. He closed the door, sat at his desk, and picked up the phone.

""Hi, Bill? Hi, this is Jeremy Mercer – you remember, we shared a ward while you were having your heart bypass ten years ago? It's been a while, eh? … No, it's fine – I'm not surprised you don't remember me – you were on pretty strong meds. So was I for that matter. How's the wife? … Well, I'm sorry to hear that. And the kids? … Sorry to hear that too. Anyway, maybe this'll put a smile on your face. Those drugs we were on seemed to have knocked this out of my mind, but I only just remembered I owe you ten dollars. Just let me know your address – I'll send you a cheque … You sure? I don't mind … Well, that's awfully generous of you … Me? Oh, I'm a politician … Yeah, look me up online. Jeremy Mercer. Ignore the whole "Gardener" thing – that was a smear campaign. The election's not for a couple of years, but I trust I can rely on your vote. Ha! Ha! Just a joke – you "follow your heart," so to speak. We'll have to catch up again soon. Later, Bill."

"More calls of a similar nature followed. Some were less than friendly, but apparently most of the people Mercer called were happy to chat. Most people declined his offer of the ten dollar cheque, but now and again he'd take down a postal address, pretending he didn't have it printed in front of him.

"A few hours later, he returned to the shredder. I braced myself for the onslaught. Hopefully this wouldn't take long. The grating sound from the mechanism was still ringing in my ears from the previous day.

"Then, against all probably, two words flashed before my eyes on the title page of a document just before it was sliced into strips. It was my own name. Clearly my records were being discarded on the grounds that I didn't have a phone.

"Unable to stop myself, I burst out of the bin, spilling curled white strands all over the carpet.

""*You* again!" said Mercer.

""I lost my screwdriver," I said.

""Really?"

""No, not really. Are you doing what I think you're doing, Mr Mercer?"

""What do *you* think I'm doing?"

""Are you seriously going to phone every single registered voter in the city pretending you know them?

""Of course not," said Mercer. "That would be ridiculous. There are *millions* of registered voters."

""So what are you doing?"

""I'm calling the *floating* voters. There's no point contacting the ones who are definitely going to vote for me or the ones that definitely aren't. I've paid a substantial sum to a data company to give me the lowdown on everyone else. My advisers have calculated that the election can be swung by as little as ten or twenty thousand. Do you know how many voters I'll get to speak to if I make a hundred calls a day over the course of two years?"

""Frankly, Mr Mercer, I can't be bothered to do the maths."

""Seventy three thousand," he said. "It's a lot of work, but in anyone's book, that's a *landslide*."

""And you're actually sending out ten dollar cheques to anyone who takes up your offer?"

""I've budgeted for it," he said. "And before you make an accusation, it's not bribery. To them, it's a repayment on a loan – the act of a trustworthy individual."

""Don't you have anything better to do?" I said.

""Not really. I could try winning votes through doing my job, but I've seen too many MPs lose their seats that way."

""You're a terrible human being," I said.

""If you don't like me," said Mercer, "I suggest you leave me alone."

"And so, I did. I could hardly spy on him after that, and having witnessed him at work, I wasn't sure I could take any more. Believe it or not, fellow eavesdropper, I have moral standards. Make of that what you will. My throat's getting tired."

As The Observer made his way towards the exit, Lester let out a muffled sneeze.

"Bless you," said The Observer, and disappeared.

33

"Did I do anything wrong?" said Lester. "Listening to those stories?"

"No one got hurt," said Eliza.

"What about the *principle?*"

"I thought about this a lot when I was doing the whole Slumber Fairy thing," said Eliza. "It all seemed so inconsequential. No one ever knew I was there."

"I never quite know what to make of morality," said Lester. "Everything seems to be a toss-up between good and evil. How am I supposed to differentiate between the two?"

"I'm not sure that's how morality works," said Eliza.

"What's the deal then?"

"Let's put it this way: some things are good, some things are bad, but mainly things are just *things*. Sitting on the roof listening to stories – that's just a thing."

"Even so," said Lester, "I don't think I can do it anymore."

"Whatever works for you."

"Maybe I can avoid morality altogether – stick to the things that are just things."

"What about your stories?" said Eliza. "Do they serve any moral purpose?"

"I hope not."

"Why?"

"I'm not sure I could handle the responsibility."

"Tell me a story," she said. "One with a moral message."

"Hmmm," said Lester, and gazed into space for a while. "There's one about a guy who sleepwalked. I *think* it has a moral. As I say, I can never be sure."

"Tell me. I'll be the judge."

"OK."

34

There was an electrical engineer who was in possession of a rare form of sleepwalking. His condition caused him to live an entirely different life while unconscious. His name was Brendon Melt.

Brendon lived on Jennifer's 17th floor and worked night shifts making car batteries in one of the city's few remaining factories.

Unbeknownst to him, during daylight hours, he would regularly wander out of his apartment and drive to the Clean City where his sleeping self owned a large house.

The sleepwalking Brendon had the ability to pass himself off as a regular citizen. He could hold meaningful conversations and establish close friendships. Having been granted free access to his own subconscious, he was able to tap into super-intelligent areas of his brain that his waking self kept firmly locked away. After a series of cunning investments, he'd grown to become one of the richest men in the city.

All the while, Brendon's waking self trundled on making car batteries in the night. It wasn't too bad a job, all in all. He liked the quiet. He enjoyed the relentless repetition of spark after spark, wire after wire.

He wondered why he was so tired all the time. The fact that he stayed up all night didn't fully explain it. As far as he was concerned, he slept perfectly well during the day, despite any racket the neighbours might happen to be making.

He didn't pay much attention to the news. One of his workmates mentioned to him that there was a mysterious business tycoon who was also called Brendon Melt.

"Another me?" said Brendon. "Ha! Ha! That's hilarious."

"Yeah," said his workmate. "God help us, eh?"

"Ha! Ha! Ha!"

While the sleeping Brendon was fully in control of his actions, the part of him that remained asleep was always compelled to deposit himself back to his bed on Jennifer's 17th floor. He'd begin to feel hazy at around eight in the evening. Whatever he happened to be doing, whether he was dining out with friends, or talking business with his overseas contacts, he would stop and wander robot-like to his car before driving back to the Dirty City.

There was a moment one afternoon when Brendon inadvertently woke up. He was standing in a room filled with bankers in fancy dress. It was the middle of the day. A woman dressed as a rhino was calling the room to order. She was auctioning off a box that apparently used to be one of Defo Tresor's stage suits.

He passed out. Shortly afterwards, his sleeping self opened his eyes, stood up and returned to the charity auction, unaware that the mishap had even taken place.

That night, Brendon told his workmate about the incident.

"You know what it means, don't you?" said his workmate.

"No. What does it mean?"

His workmate laughed. "It means you were *dreaming*."

"Interesting," said Brendon. "I never remember my dreams."

"Oh right," said his workmate.

"What do you mean?"

"I didn't say anything."

"You said "Oh right.""

"So?"

"Just wondering what you meant," said Brendon.

"Well, I'm no psychologist," said his workmate, "but they say that if you can't remember your dreams it means you're massively repressed in some way."

"Hmmm," said Brendon. "Yeah. Something to think about, eh?"

"I wouldn't think too hard about it if I were you," said his workmate. "It's the sort of thing that could drive you insane."

"Oh right."

As his alter ego's wealth increased, Brendon's work at the factory became increasingly strained. The company were struggling to compete with the multinational competition. Redundancies meant Brendon's job became twice as hard.

Brendon didn't mind all that much. He quite liked the challenge.

With each month that passed, more and more employees were laid off, leaving the remaining workforce stretched to breaking point. Still, Brendon appeared almost oblivious.

Then one day, it was announced that the company were being bought out by a local business tycoon.

Brendon's workmate heard the news before he did.

"Take a wild stab in the dark," he said. "You'll never guess who's about to take over the business."

"His initials aren't BM, by any chance?" said Brendon.

"Ha! Ha! Got it in one!"

Brendon chuckled along. "Nice one," he said. "I never thought I'd get to be my own boss!"

The merriment didn't last long. Two weeks after Brendon Melt's takeover of the motor company, it was announced that the entire workforce were to be made redundant. The factory was moving overseas to a country with cheaper labour and a slacker attitude to human rights. Brendon's waking self had never even heard of the place.

One evening not long afterwards, when eight o'clock rolled around, Brendon the tycoon sleepwalked back to his apartment on Jennifer's 17th floor, as he'd done every night for many years. He stopped as he realised he didn't have a key. Somewhere between one personality and the next, his sleeping self deduced that he no longer lived in his apartment. He'd spent the last seven nights wandering the streets, reading abandoned magazines in the park and fishing out leftover chicken tikka from restaurant bins.

Presented with the briefest flash of his waking self, the sleepwalking Brendon Melt got back in his car and returned to his house in the Clean City. He climbed the stairs, and visited a part of the house he'd never even set foot in – the bedroom.

He slept soundly for several days.

On waking, he continued living his life as though nothing unusual had happened. Technically, he was still asleep.

It was a rare occasion on which Brendon would wander the streets, but one night an overwhelming sense of restlessness sent the sleepwalking Brendon out into the moonlight.

He wandered for hours, weaving his way between anonymous office blocks, and slipping down pitch-black alleyways for no particular reason.

While passing a park bench, a voice called out – "Oi, Brendon!"

Under normal circumstances, Brendon would've been inclined to ignore the mention of his name, assuming it to be one of the many disgruntled members of the public who'd happily have seen him dead. But the voice sounded familiar.

He turned.

"Alright?" said the guy on the bench.

"Do I know you?" said Brendon.

"'Course you know me. We worked together."

He half-recognised his old workmate's face.

"I think you might be mistaking me for someone else."

"Another Brendon Melt?" said his old workmate. "Hey – maybe you're Brendon Melt the billionaire."

"I *am* Brendon Melt the billionaire."

"You don't look like Brendon Melt the billionaire."

"Why? What does Brendon Melt the billionaire look like?"

"Dunno. All I know is, there's an electrical engineer named Brendon Melt who looks exactly like you."

"Oh right," said Brendon.

"What do you mean "Oh right"?"

"You've got a point," said Brendon thoughtfully. "I *am* Brendon Melt the electrical engineer, aren't I? But I'm dreaming."

"No you're not."

"How do you know?"

"Because this is real life."

"How do you know you're not just a figment of my imagination?"

"Because I'm not. How long have you been dreaming for?"

"Difficult to say. It's one of those dreams that seems like it's been going on for years."

"Or maybe you're just living the kind of life most of us can only dream of."

"I'm a little confused."

"So am I, Brendon, truth be told."

"Maybe I should see someone about it."

"Maybe you should."

And so, Brendon visited his doctor. The doctor called a sleep specialist from Clean City University who ran some tests. Then she hired a private detective.

After a period of extensive research, the doctor and her team sat down with Brendon and broke the news.

"Brendon," she said, "there's no simple way of saying this, but I'll state it as plainly as possible. You're asleep."

"I know," said Brendon. "That's why I came."

"Technically you're completely unconscious twenty-four hours a day."

"I know."

"To be perfectly honest, we've never encountered this particular disorder before."

"So you don't know how to treat it?"

"No, we know how to treat it."

"Are you going to tell me?"

"It's simple, Brendon," said the doctor. "We wake you up."

"Are you *serious?*" he snapped. "If it's that simple, then what's all the fuss about? Wake me up. I've got meetings to attend."

"It's not as simple as that," said the doctor.

"Why not?"

"Can you remember anything about your waking self, Brendon?"

"Not really," he said. "I know I make car batteries."

"*Used* to make car batteries," growled a man in the corner, "until you laid yourself off."

"Who's this guy?" said Brendon.

"My name's Wilks," said the man.

"He's a private investigator," said the doctor.

"What's he doing here?"

"Assisting me with the diagnosis. He's been conducting some research into your waking self."

"And a fine example of a man he was too," said Wilks. "Simple, modest, gentle. All the things you're not. Yes, he may have been poor, but he was happy! Happier than you, I dare say."

"I'm quite happy," said Brendon.

"'Course you're happy – you're the richest man in the city. Your waking self was content even when he was the poorest."

Brendon shrugged. "Bit tricky to define happiness, I suppose," he said.

"Let's simplify it," said the doctor. "Brendon, you're faced with a choice. Do we wake you up, or do we keep you asleep? If we wake you up, you'll be your old self again. If we keep you asleep, you'll continue as you are."

"I don't really fancy getting rid of me," said Brendon. "It'd be rather like suicide."

"So, you're saying...?"

"Yes. Decision made. I'd like to carry on dreaming, if that's OK."

"NO!" barked Wilks, leaping to his feet. "It's *not* OK!" He grabbed Brendon by the shoulders. "WAKE UP!" he screamed in his face. "WAKE UP!"

It took a minute or so for the hospital security to prise the Wilks's fingers from Brendon's body.

"Sorry about that," said the doctor. "Looks like I'll have to be more selective next time I call in outside help..."

She stopped talking as she realised Brendon was no longer there. Amidst the commotion, he'd risen from his slumber, and wandered out of the hospital.

She found him in the car park, examining grey sky above him as though it were a crossword puzzle.

35

As it happened, Wilks was himself under observation by a private investigator called Sandra.

One morning at 3am, Sandra received an email offering her a thousand dollars a day to find out as much information as possible about her target.

She picked up the message at breakfast a few hours later. *"What kind of information?"* she typed back.

The response appeared at 3am the following morning. *"Find out whatever you can about Wilks's internal world."*

Sandra specialised in exposing unfaithful partners, or uncovering the dodgy tax accounts of her clients' enemies. She didn't consider herself qualified to discover a person's internal world, but grand-a-day cases didn't come along very often.

Sandra's long-standing tactic was to befriend the person she was investigating in order to extract information. This seemed a good enough place to start.

Wilks was eating a sandwich in a café when Sandra sat down opposite him.

"Is this seat taken?" she said.

Wilks undertook a quick survey, noting there were plenty of unoccupied tables.

"It's fine," he said.

Sandra reached for the menu. "I've never eaten here before," she said. "What would you recommend?"

"You're asking the wrong guy," said Wilks. "I will literally eat *anything*."

They laughed.

"*Anything*?" she said.

"Afraid so. I've got a habit of scavenging from bins when I'm low on cash."

It seemed like a perfectly natural thing to say. Under any other circumstances, revealing one of his most embarrassing secrets to a total stranger would've come as an unpleasant surprise, but there was something indescribably special about Sandra's face.

"I'll have what you're having," she said.

#

Several lunch dates followed. Sandra was quick to pretend she was married, so their relationship needed to remain strictly platonic. Wilks was disappointed, but happy to go along with their arrangement. Sandra was the most perfect human being he'd ever met. Just spending time in her company was enough.

After several dates, Sandra wrote an email response to her mysterious client:

I've gathered whatever I can, she typed. *Wilks is dedicated to his work – much more so than I am, as it turns out. He'll only ever spy on someone genuinely corrupt. He's passionate about doing the right thing, and has been known to experience fits of rage in the face of injustice. You probably know this, but he's the guy who woke up Brendon Melt. Anyway.*

He's a loner. He'll often go for days without speaking to a soul. Sometimes he invites homeless people back to his apartment, providing them with food and board for as long as they need before moving on to places of their own. He'd like to do it more often, but as I say, he likes to be alone. At the same time, there's a part of Wilks that craves companionship. I guess that's why he's been so happy to continue seeing me.

That's your lot, I'm afraid. I don't suppose I've told you a great deal about Wilks's internal world, but sadly I'm going to have to pull out of this case. I take pride in my work, but I can't go on deceiving this man. If you really want to know, I'm beginning to fall in love with him.

I don't suppose this was worth a thousand dollars a day. In fact, I've reversed the bank transfer as I don't feel I can accept your money.

I hope you find what you're looking for, whatever your reasons.

Regards,

Sandra

#

The following morning, Wilks woke up in his desk chair, having fallen asleep in bed.

"Must've been sleepwalking," he muttered.

He glanced at his watch. It was 3am.

On the computer screen in front of him was an email. It read: *I've gathered whatever I can…*

36

In one isolated section of the Dirty City, there was a phenomenon known as "synchronised sleepwalking." Specifically, the condition affected Jennifer's inhabitants on floors 16 to 38.

Each of Jennifer's storeys was composed of ten apartments. The layout of each apartment varied, but the building was designed in such a way that each apartment was identical to the one immediately below it.

The mass act relied on the inhabitants of each apartment being asleep at the same time. It was a rare occurrence but occasionally every single insomniac, stargazer and party animal between floors 16 to 38 was blissfully unconscious. This usually occurred around 3am.

Once everyone was sleeping soundly, the performance began. Each sleepwalker would rise from their beds, couches or hammocks. They would get dressed, slip into their shoes and exit the apartment, leaving the door unlocked. They would descend the stairs to the apartment immediately below. To complete the circle, the inhabitants of floor 16 would take the lifts up to floor 38.

Once inside their neighbours' apartments, they would make themselves at home in whatever way they saw fit. They'd cook dinner. They'd rearrange the furniture. They'd graffiti the walls. They'd help themselves to any cash or valuables they found lying around. Then, on an unspoken signal, every single sleepwalking inhabitant of floors 16 to 38 would stop what they were doing, leave their neighbours' apartments and climb the stairs, returning to their own beds.

The following morning, the sleepwalkers awoke with the memory of a dream in which they were hovering in the air outside the building. The building and its contents were transparent. All that was visible were the people themselves. While hovering, the sleepwalkers observed themselves descending the stairs and ransacking their neighbours' properties, while all around them the same pattern was repeated.

Half-conscious, Jennifer herself had the same dream. For all concerned, their out of body experience seemed hauntingly realistic.

#

One morning, one of the inhabitants of Jennifer's 26th floor awoke on their sofa to find a message scrawled across her carpet – "WE SHOULD MOVE IN TOGETHER. SPLIT THE RENT." They were written in mustard.

For the girl in question, this was the fourteenth time an attack of synchronised sleepwalking had occurred – roughly once a month since she'd moved in just over a year previously. This was the first time anyone had offered to move in with her.
She was running late for work, so didn't have time to think about the message. She didn't even have time to clean it up. Returning home after a twelve hour shift, all she wanted to do was flop into bed and sleep. On stepping through the door, she remembered the place had been mysteriously vandalised by whoever was living in the upstairs apartment.

    She climbed the stairs and knocked on the stranger's door.
    The stranger answered.
    "Hi," he said.
    "Do I know you?" she said.
    "Don't think so," he said. "What can I do for you?"
    "Did you write the words "We should move in together" on my carpet?"
    "Probably," he said. "The landlord warned me about this "synchronised sleepwalking" thing. Apparently it comes with the property."
    "So, this is your first time?"
    "Yeah. Looks like I put my foot in it."
    "It's OK – you'll get used to it."
    "Sorry."
    "No need to apologise."
    "What did I use, anyway?"
    "How do you mean?"
    "I mean, what did I write "We should move in together" with?"
    "Mustard."
    "Funny. I love mustard."
    "You love mustard? Great. Maybe we should move in together, split the rent and share the mustard."
    They laughed.
    A couple of days later they went out for a drink. They enjoyed each others' company. He moved into her apartment the following weekend.
    Four weeks later, the girl returned home after a night shift at the restaurant to find her apartment trashed. She wasn't in any way surprised.
    She made herself some toast and a cup of coffee.
    She was about to start clearing up the room when the doorbell rang.
    She answered the door.
    "Hello," she said. "Can I help you?"
    "Do you live here?" said the woman at the door.
    "I'm guessing you're from the apartment downstairs. Sorry, we haven't been introduced yet."
    "I don't know what stunt you're trying to pull..."

"Sorry," said the girl. "Are you new in the building? You may not have been told..."

"I know all about it, thanks," said the woman. "Synchronised sleepwalking – they filled me in – but I wasn't expecting..."

"Sorry," said the girl. "I wasn't actually here last night."

"Clearly someone was."

"Ah. That'll be my flatmate."

"Oh, he's *your* flatmate, is he? Well, he just suggested that the two of us should move in together and split the rent."

"He said what?"

"Oh, he didn't actually say it verbally," said the woman. "He wrote it on my bathroom wall in mayonnaise."

#

As it turns out, the man had been offering to move in with his neighbours since he moved into his original apartment on the 38th floor. Over the last year, he'd flat-hopped his way down twelve flights of stairs.

"Don't blame me," was his simple defence. "Blame our collective unconscious."

"I'd rather blame *you*, thanks," said the girl.

"Fine," he said. "I can see this isn't working out. Maybe I should move downstairs..."

37

There was an apartment on the 44th floor inhabited by one hundred and seven people. They each occupied a person-sized rectangle of floor space. They had no possessions other than a pillow, a blanket, and a small baggage allowance. Some erected their own tents.

The rent on the apartment was one hundred and seven dollars a week. The flatmates had disposed of the entire contents of the kitchen to make room for more rectangles. Paying a dollar a week in rent meant that each inhabitant could afford to eat out for every single meal. They joined a gym so that they had a place to shower. The only housework anyone ever had to do was to clean up their own floor space.

Power in numbers kept arguments to a minimum. If anyone was caught making too much noise or encroaching on another flatmate's floor space, the collective soon put a stop to it.

Group guidelines stated that friends could only visit during daylight hours, and only when the apartment was at least 50% empty.

Whenever outsiders were permitted to enter, they were amazed at the sight that greeted them as they entered.

Some were sceptical. "You've ripped out all the furnishings," they said. "The only thing left is the bath, and even then you've got someone sleeping in it. How do you expect to get your deposit back?"

"We won't," they said. "We'll always be here. Some will leave, others will arrive, but there will always be one hundred and seven people living in this apartment."

The apartment's inhabitants became such a close-knit community that they applied for their apartment to be classified as a separate country with its own laws.

The Government declined the proposal, and alerted the authorities on the assumption that the apartment was occupied by a group of dangerous subversives. Shortly afterwards, at least three of the apartment's newer inhabitants were undercover police officers. They were no harm to anyone.

The inhabitants' next brainwave was to open up a joint savings account. Each member agreed to pay a proportion of their income on a monthly basis. A lot of the flatmates had relatively well-paid jobs – lawyers, accountants, university professors. Even the undercover cops paid in. It wasn't long before the group saved enough to purchase their own apartment in the trendiest part of the Clean City.

As their friends had predicted, they didn't get their deposit back.

38

There was a man who could have conversations with concepts.
    He talked to guilt about shame behind shame's back.
    He talked to the mind about its relationship with the body.
    He had a discussion with bewilderment about chess moves.
    He had a conversation with the concept of language composed entirely of words he'd made up on the spot.
    He regularly discussed the concept of music with music itself.
    One unusually foggy night, Lester was sitting on the ground just outside Jennifer when he heard the man's voice yelling down through one of the 7th floor windows. The man appeared to be addressing an unknown force hovering somewhere in the mist.
    "Isn't it so deeply ironic?" he shouted. "You abandoned me at my most vulnerable moment, not even having the courtesy to transmigrate into a lesser form as a source of comfort. I hate you. Ha! How deeply ironic. I hate you. I hate you. I hate you."
    "Hello," called Lester.
    "Oh," called the man. "Hello."
    "Who are you shouting at?"
    The man grinned bitterly. "*Love*, of course. Who else?"
    "Right," said Lester. "I've heard of that. Can't quite get my head around it."
    "Stay away," said the man firmly.
    "Why?" said Lester.
    "It's not worth it."
    "I've heard people say things like that, then I've heard the same people say the opposite. It just doesn't make any sense to me."
    "It doesn't make sense to *anyone* – that's the problem. Ever tried having a conversation with it?"
    "With what? Love?"
    "Yeah."
    "I'd have to find it first, and I'm not sure that I want to."
    "*Don't,*" said the man. "Seriously. Don't bother."
    "Thanks for the tip," said Lester. "I'll bear that in mind."

39

"What do you think about love?" said Lester.

"It's a concept," said Eliza.

"Do you *feel* it?"

"In what way?"

"Dunno. I don't really understand my own question."

"Hmmm," said Eliza. "If I do "feel love," whatever that means, it isn't for a specific person or group. It's for *everything*."

"Everything in the universe, or…?"

"Well, I can't speak for the universe as a whole. Maybe I just love the Dirty City."

"Every single person?"

"Not exactly. I don't hang around with people that much. Maybe I'm in love with myself."

"*I* certainly am. With myself, I mean."

"So, you couldn't imagine yourself – you know – being in love with someone else?"

"What does that even mean?"

"I don't know. It all seems like far too much effort."

"Agreed."

"So, what shall we do now?"

"Nothing."

"Sounds good to me."

40

Owing to her superhuman reflexes, Eliza considered herself to be the one person in the city who'd never get mugged. So, one evening when she suddenly found herself flat on her back on the blotchy pavement, she was more surprised than the average citizen would've been. Her mouth remained open for several minutes.

The mugging itself was over in the blink of an eye. It was a highly professional job, clearly committed by a soft-hearted criminal. The attack may have been executed at high speed, but Eliza was gently eased to the ground, to the extent that she felt no pain. If she was going to be mugged, she couldn't have chosen a more respectful criminal.

Once she'd regained control of her speech, Eliza cancelled her credit cards and – for the first time in her life – paid a visit to a police station.

She was introduced to a police officer with an inappropriately wide grin.

"Call me Spool," he said.

"Eliza," she said.

"Good to meet you."

"I'd like to say the same, but I'm not in the best of moods."

"Don't worry," he said. "I'll show you something that'll cheer you up."

He invited her into a dark room filled with small TV screens.

"The bad news is, you've been mugged," said Spool.

"I kind of knew that."

"The good news is, there's a new form of surveillance technology known as AIVC."

Eliza glanced at her watch, wondering how long she'd have to spend in the grinning man's presence. "Never heard of it," she said.

Spool lowered his tone a little. "You're not supposed to. But I like you."

"Why?"

"I don't know. Something about your face."

"Tell me then. What does AIVC stand for?"

"Automated Interpretative Video Capture. I don't know why they have to give these things such terrible names."

"What does it do?"

"I'll show you."

Spool logged into his computer and quickly located the details of the AIVC cameras in the area Eliza had been attacked.

On one of the TV screens appeared an image of Eliza being dragged to the ground. According to the footage, she'd been mugged by a giant eagle.

"Oh," she said. "Well, that's explains it."

The corners of Spool's lips straightened out momentarily. "I thought you might be surprised," he said.

"You like impressing people with this thing, don't you?"

"You're not shocked by the idea of having your credit cards stolen by a bird?"

"Makes perfect sense," said Eliza. "No human being could've caught me unawares like that."

Spool pressed another button. On another screen, the video was played out from a different angle. This time she was dragged to the ground by a seven year-old child on a skateboard.

Eliza let out a stifled gasp.

"You see why I like impressing people with this?" said Spool.

He pressed another button. The image of Eliza being mugged was played out from a camera positioned directly above the incident. This time the attack was carried out by a bolt of lightning.

Eliza resisted the urge to slap Spool across the face. "Are you going to stop messing about and tell me who stole my wallet?" she said.

"I don't know," said Spool. "It's not my job to know either. The camera doesn't see what we see. Camera number one personified the attacker as an eagle, interpreting their actions as a deadly, calculated assault. Camera number two portrayed the attacker as a child because from its psychoanalytical perspective, the attack was provoked by the frustrations of the mugger's inner child. I've got no idea what camera number three was playing at. Trying to be clever, possibly."

"I don't really understand the purpose of all this," said Eliza. "Are you telling me you don't know what this person physically looks like?"

"The question is, which works better – a picture of a hooded kid who could've been anyone, or a camera with a unique insight into the hooded kid's mind?" He pointed at the first screen. "That's not an eagle – that's the equivalent of a fingerprint."

"So, what are you supposed to do now? Hunt for an eagle?"

"Me? I won't be doing anything. The cameras will track Eagle Boy down. All I need to do is highlight these three images, press this button here, and there you go – the report has been sent. From this moment, every other AIVC camera in the city will be looking for an individual who matches this profile. I'll be sitting back with a coffee and a sausage roll. Want one?"

"I'm vegetarian," she said, "but I'll take a coffee."

"Coming right up."

Spool paused halfway through standing up. He slumped back into his seat with a thoughtful expression.

"Are you sure you weren't impressed by the cameras? They usually knock 'em dead, so to speak."

"It's alright," said Eliza. "Bit of a gimmick if you ask me."

"Fine," said Spool. "Forget the coffee. Let me impress you."

"Always in the mood to be impressed," said Eliza.

"Let's go."

41

Before she had chance to question the sanity of her actions, Eliza found herself in the passenger seat of a police car, being escorted up the rickety road to Mile Prison.

"This place is just for the hardcore criminals," Spool explained as they drove. "You may not be pleased to hear this, but once Eagle Boy is apprehended – which shouldn't be too much longer – he'll be hit with an affordable fine and sent on his way. Unless he's a serial offender, this place'll be out of bounds."

"Why are you taking me to jail?" said Eliza.

"Some male cops try to impress girls with their guns. I don't go in for that."

"Oh, so you're trying to impress me in *that* way?"

Spool shrugged. "Why not?"

"As long as you manage to genuinely impress me, I don't care," said Eliza. "You may have gathered, I've seen a few too many extraordinarily things in my time."

They arrived at the looming gates, and were ushered in by a security guard who looked like he'd been drinking solidly since the previous night. Spool parked up as the gates clanked shut.

"Let's try a little role play," he said. "Imagine you're being sentenced to life imprisonment."

"I'd rather not," said Eliza. "It's one of my all-time worst fears." Her eyes darted up at the sealed gates towering over them. "Hang on," she said. "If this is some kind of *stitch-up*..."

Spool smiled. "Why? What've you done?"

Eliza managed to look convincingly innocent. "Nothing," she said. "Just got paranoid for a second."

"OK, so imagine you're facing life behind bars. The gates have slammed shut. Now follow me. Imagine I'm showing you to your new permanent residence."

He led her across the empty car park to a set of enormous white doors.

"Why does everything have to be so *big?*" she said.

"For effect," he said. "Simple as that."

Spool pushed open the unlocked door, and turned on the lights.

One by one, a series of ceiling strips illuminated themselves to reveal a grand hall, boasting row after row of unlocked cells. The place was painted purest white. There wasn't a speck of dust to be seen.

"Go on," said Spool.

"I don't understand," said Eliza.

"Incomprehension," he said. "That's the first stage."

"There's *no one here.*"

"Evidently."

"Have I seriously just been escorted into an empty prison?"

Spool's smug grin widened. "I wouldn't say "empty." There's the alcoholic who operates the gate, plus we get a team of cleaners in once a week. They do a remarkable job, don't you think?"

This time, Eliza actually did slap him across the face. Unfortunately Spool seemed to enjoy it.

"Anger," he said. "Stage two."

"Oh, shut up."

"I don't think you want me to shut up," said Spool. "How else will you get an explanation?"

"Go on then. Make it brief. I'm sick of your voice."

Spool's expression wavered a little. His attempts at making a good impression clearly hadn't gone as well as he'd hoped.

"How much do you know about the history of this city?" he said.

"Tons," said Eliza. "I like history."

"Is that because you like stories?"

"Everyone likes stories, don't they?"

"You in particular."

"How do you know?"

"I can tell, that's all."

"So, you think you know more about history than me?"

"Do you know about the civilisations that existed before this one?"

"What civilisations?"

"I'll take that as a no."

"OK," said Eliza, arms folded. *"Impress* me."

"Take a seat," he said.

42

"Legend has it, there are three dead civilisations buried beneath our own. I'll tell you a story about each. None of these events actually took place, but each story contains at least a grain of truth. I'll begin with the most ridiculous."

"Even more ridiculous than *this?*" Eliza waved her arms at the bare white walls.

"What I mean is, you'll hear this story and you'll wonder why I'm trying to pass this off as history. Bear in mind, this account was shared with me because I was as baffled as you are."

"Go on then."

"OK."

#

The industrialised kingdom buried beneath the Dirty City collapsed as the result of a catastrophic legal and ethical experiment.

Upon the death of a tyrant king, his newly-crowned daughter's first act was to abolish the death penalty. The Queen declared that although she held absolute power over the city, she should not be granted the right to kill her own subjects.

Her closest adviser was her Deputy Butler, who offered some stern advice while polishing a TV cabinet. "How are we supposed to punish criminals or protect society from thieves and murderers?" he said.

She said, "I've been doing some research into the dead civilisation buried beneath this one. They had this thing called a *prison*."

"A what?"

"The principle is, you lock the criminals away to protect society from harm."

"Instead of just executing them?"

"It's a matter of principle. Since I was a young girl, I've been formulating a simple set of rules in anticipation of the day I'd find myself in charge. Rule number one – don't kill people. Rule number two – practise what you preach."

"So, who's going to cover the cost of all this? The *taxpayer?* You'd be overthrown in a matter of days."

"Well, why don't we place the decision in the hands of the people? They can vote."

"Ma'am, are you sure you're feeling well?"

"It's a compromise," said the Queen. "Either we put it to the vote, or we abolish it altogether."

"Then let's compromise," said the Deputy Butler. "For the love of sanity."

And so, a vote was cast. The people of the city had two options: either a prison system be introduced, or the death penalty be kept in place. The option of the death penalty came with a clause: if a person is executed, the person who executed them must be executed too. As the Queen suggested, it was only fair.

The results of the vote came in later that day. The overwhelming majority of the general public voted in favour of the death penalty.

The new law was passed with immediate effect.

The Queen was speechless for days.

A week later, her Deputy Butler visited her at her bedside.

"It's not my place to say, Ma'am," he said, "but perhaps it's time to get out of bed."

The Queen finally broke her silence. "Why?" she said. "Don't these people understand anything? Was the small print not large enough for them?"

"It seems they understand perfectly, Ma'am."

"How do you mean?"

"If I may say so, Ma'am, this is the greatest policy anyone has ever had the courage to implement. Well done."

"Listen," she said, "I know you're a fan of capital punishment. There's no need to rub my nose in it."

"You misunderstand me, Ma'am. Do you realise that since the new law was passed, no one has committed a crime of any kind?"

"Why not?"

"Too scared, Ma'am. Facing the death penalty means being responsible for the demise of everyone else in the city. If their executioner is obliged to be killed, that person's executioner will be killed as well, until the domino effect wipes out the entire population. No one, not even the wildest of psychopaths, wishes to become the person responsible for killing the entire city. Ma'am, you've single-handedly destroyed all forms of crime."

"Have I?"

"Yes."

"You don't think this is just a tiny bit risky?"

"No, Ma'am. It's pure genius."

#

Years passed. As the Deputy Butler had predicted, not even the most nihilistic inhabitants of the city were willing to wipe out the entire human population.

One day, a car mechanic named Eric Sycamore had the bright idea of committing a crime for which he'd never be prosecuted. He'd murder his wife Samantha and pass it off as an accident.

Thinking about it, he was sure that many, many people had murdered their friends, enemies and relatives without anyone suspecting. That's what this new form of capital punishment represented: it wasn't a deterrent – it was an encouragement, if one were needed, not to get caught.

Considering that the city's police force had been virtually disbanded, it seemed like a fairly straightforward task.

As it turned out, Eric Sycamore was one of the world's least subtle attempted murderers. His plan had been to kill Samantha by pushing her into the path of a speeding truck in such a way as to make it appear like an accident.

Perhaps his plan would've succeeded were it not for the fact that he committed the crime in broad daylight in the middle of a crowded street, in clear view of one of the city's few remaining police patrol cars.

Halfway through a shopping trip, Eric successfully managed to shove his wife into the path of an oncoming vehicle.

A few seconds after the driver slammed on the breaks, Samantha was ever so gently nudged to the ground, administering a slight graze to her forearm.

As Eric fled the scene, a helpful passerby managed to wrestle him to the ground.

The hero paused as he pinned Eric's arm behind his back.

He looked up.

The street had fallen silent. All eyes were on him.

He noticed that not a single person had volunteered to assist him – not even the police officers, who appeared to be making a hasty retreat.

This may have been a clear case of attempted murder, but handing the perpetrator over to the authorities would've resulted in the deaths of every single man, woman and child in the city.

"Nah," the hero muttered. "Not worth it."

He let go of Eric's arm and kicked him as hard as he could in the stomach.

He stepped away.

The street remained silent.

There was a minute of communal consideration.

Then it started.

#

The Queen was awoken from her afternoon nap by her Deputy Butler.

"Ma'am," he said softly.

"Mmmm?" said the Queen.

"I'm not sure how to tell you this, but…"

"What's that noise?"

"Rioting, Ma'am. It's been going on for a couple of hours."

"Sounds awfully close."

"We're being burgled, Ma'am. We don't have sufficient security. They've taken most of the silverware."

"What happened?"

"It would appear that crime has been reintroduced, rather violently."

"Oh."

"Indeed."

The Queen sat up in bed, quietly considering her next move. "Has anyone done anything really bad?" she said. "I mean, pinching a bit of silver, maybe we can forgive…"

"You mean has anyone done anything to warrant the death penalty?" said the Deputy Butler.

"Yes."

The Deputy Butler gazed at the impeccably polished floor. "According to the rumours," he said, "there have been a number of deaths."

The Queen reached for her crown, which was waiting for her by the bedside. She hooked it carefully into her hair. "We'd better proceed," she said.

"Ma'am," said the Butler. "Consider your actions carefully. The reason your subjects are rioting in the first place is because they know it would be insane for anyone in this city to make an arrest. There isn't a single police officer who'd be willing to do it."

"Then I'll do it myself," said the Queen.

#

The blast of destructive activity that began a couple of hours previously had begun to die down when the Queen and her awkward gaggle of guards stepped into the street.

At the sight of the most praised and respected leader in history, the rioters had no option but to bow their heads in hushed shame.

The Queen wandered through the streets. Wherever she stepped, her subjects responded in the same apologetic manner.

After a while, the Queen caught sight of a man who'd been strung up by his feet, and was hanging upside down from a lamppost. His groan indicated that he was still conscious.

"Who are you?" said the Queen.

"Eric Sycamore, Ma'am."

"And why have my subjects gone to the trouble of tying your feet to the top of a lamppost? Must've taken a while."

"Indeed it did, Ma'am," Sycamore winced.

"Did you do anything to deserve it?"

"Indeed I did, Ma'am."

"What did you do?"

"Tried to murder my wife."

"I see," said the Queen. "It pains me to say so, Mr Sycamore, but you're under arrest. Let's skip the trial and get to the point. You'll be executed shortly."

"Thank you, Ma'am."

#

And so, one by one, the Queen's subjects were killed. The guards had the city fenced off and surrounded. Anyone caught attempting to leave were shot on sight. The Queen watched straight-faced as one citizen after another was forced to play the role of executioner.

Softly, a voice said, "Ma'am?"

"Yes?" said the Queen.

"It's not too late to stop. Please. Surely you can see the horror you've instigated. Surely you remember the rules you formulated as a young girl. *Don't kill people*. That was rule number one."

"Practise what you preach," said the Queen. "That was the second."

"You're obeying neither of those rules."

"I relinquished the right to administer justice," said the Queen. "I granted power to the people. I gave them the right to select their fate. They made the wrong choice."

"But don't you see?" said the Deputy Butler. "You have the power to reverse it."

"I'm sorry," said the Queen. "It's my turn now."

The Deputy Butler turned to see a lone man with a smoking gun, quivering amongst the mounds of fallen bodies.

"The only one left," said the Queen.

She stepped forward and gently removed the pistol from her subject's shaking palm.

"Must you?" said the Deputy Butler.

"I'm following the rules."

"No, you're not."

Moments later, the quivering man lay motionless on the ground. The Queen handed the gun to her Deputy Butler.

"Take it," she said. "Finish the job, then go. You're the final man alive. I grant you your freedom. Kill me, then flee the city. Spread the story of our fate."

"Is that why you've done this?" said the Butler. "You wanted to tell a *story*?"

"Maybe," said the Queen. "Come on, get on with it."

"You don't know what you're saying, Ma'am."

"Do it!"

So, he did.

#

"The butler failed in his mission to spread the story to the world," said Spool. "He told very few people, and even fewer believed him. He died shortly afterwards."

He took a breath.

Eliza uncrossed her arms.

"Are you actually telling me everyone in the city was killed apart from one *butler*?"

"Almost," said Spool. "There was one man who managed to remain undetected. He outlived the butler by a long stretch. He's still alive, in fact. The oldest man in the world. Appropriately enough, he lives on Jennifer's 100th floor."

"I thought you said none of this was true."

"It's all fiction apart from the last part."

"You mean the part about the oldest man in the world?"

"Yes, but that's a digression," said Spool. "It doesn't explain the empty prison."

"It certainly doesn't."

"That involves going back even further in time."

"Fine."

43

As the dead Queen suggested, the concept of prison was invented by the civilisation that was buried below them – a dictatorship whose technological advancements were way more advanced than the present day.

In an echo of science fiction stories that were yet to be written, the society's surveillance technology had the ability to detect crimes before they'd even been committed. As soon as the possibility of engaging in some form of criminal activity entered a person's head, they were immediately transported to a secure underground cell via a remote transfer. As soon as a child learned to snatch (a form of theft, and therefore a punishable offence), they'd be taken from their parents and imprisoned for life. The murderous thoughts towards the robot regime provoked by their infants' arrests meant that the parents were imprisoned almost immediately afterwards.

One day, a woman and her husband sat watching the sun disappear behind the abandoned supermarket.

"Did you see anyone today?" she said.

"How do you mean?"

"I mean, did you come into contact with another human being?"

"To be honest," he said, "it's been weeks since I saw anyone apart from you."

"You don't think...?" she said.

"I'll admit, I've been thinking..."

"Yes?"

"I guess you're thinking the same...?"

"Tell me what you're thinking first."

"You brought it up," he said.

"OK," she said. "I'm wondering if we're the only people in the entire city who aren't in prison."

"Oh," he said. "Didn't think of that."

"Why?" she said. "What were you thinking?"

"Well," he said, "seen as that supermarket's been abandoned, maybe we could..."

At that point, the man disappeared.

The woman's immediate response was – "I could *kill* him."

And with that, the final two members of their society had been transported to their inescapable underground cells.

The good news was, the concept of prison as a form of punishment – and indeed the concept of punishment itself – had not yet been conceived. Prison was there to protect society against criminals. It had been highly effective in achieving that goal – provided that you consider "society" to mean "people who aren't in prison."

Once inside, criminals were granted every luxury available to them in the outside world. There were bars, clubs, restaurants, saunas, hot pools and tanning salons for the adults. The children's prison was a giant theme park. For a short time, the prison population could almost be defined as a utopian society.

Unfortunately with every single person inside, there was no one available to bring in resources to allow these luxuries to continue. The main cause of death was being eaten by other inmates. The few survivors that remained eventually died of starvation.

Legend has it that the only survivor was a small child, who sat at the top of the rollercoaster in the children's prison poking at the ceiling with a stick. Eventually, the roof caved in.

The child climbed to safety, and wandered the face of the planet telling tales of the horrors he'd witnessed.

#

"The remains of the dead are still down there," said Spool. "There's a network of derelict prison cells buried across the length and breadth of the city. They're a matter of metres below us."

"Really?"

"Of course not."

"Not a bad story though. I like the idea of one person surviving. Nice touch."

"So do I," said Spool, "although if I'd told the story correctly, I should've mentioned there was one man who failed to get arrested in the first place. The same man who outlived the society that followed."

"The oldest man in the world?"

"Again," said Spool, "that's a digression. Let's dig deeper."

"OK."

44

In the preceding society, loners and hermits were considered to be the wisest and happiest people alive. When a member of the general public managed to get hold of a loner or a hermit, they'd ask them why they'd chosen to seal themselves away.

There were numerous responses, but the most common reply would be, "Because I love my own company. The more time I spend with other people, the less time I get to spend with myself."

The more their society progressed, the more members of the population chose to live self-sufficiently in the fields, entirely alone.

With no medical care, minimal procreation and a relaxed attitude to death ("Whatever happens happens" as one hermit aptly expressed it), the population dwindled.

Eventually, there was only one man left. As with all tales of this nature, the man was destined to flee the country and spread the word about the fate that had befallen his people. But, of course, this man was a hermit, and had no intention of doing so.

#

"Don't tell me," said Eliza. "The oldest man in the world."

"Story for another time," said Spool.

"Anyway, as interesting as this history lesson has been, this doesn't explain why our prisons are completely empty."

"Isn't it obvious?" said Spool.

"No. That's why I asked you."

"Think about it. The only way of preventing crime is to avoid all human contact. If people are going to insist on spending time in each other's company, we need to do as much as possible to persuade the population not to kill each other. So, what's the most effective deterrent? Our predecessors have proven capital punishment doesn't work. Locking people away isn't a deterrent either – our ancestors have proven that too. There's no greater deterrent than an empty prison."

"You've explained *nothing*," said Eliza. "How's an empty prison supposed to prevent crime?"

"It doesn't *prevent* crime as such," said Spool. "It nips it in the bud. Historically, prisons were there to prevent the same crimes being committed over and over again. The trouble with the old system was, people assumed that was the only solution. Locking criminals away instead of killing them was the humane approach. This, Eliza, is where humanism meets barbarism – it's where crime truly meets punishment."

He gazed at the dazzling white walls, as his words echoed throughout the room.

"Imagine you're not the victim," he said. "Imagine you're the mugger. Doesn't necessarily mean you're a bad person. Maybe you're in a desperate situation, and you feel as though stealing by force is your only means of survival. Let's say you're caught and get arrested."

Eliza had her eyes closed. "Hang on a minute," she said. "You're moving too fast. I'm still establishing my character. I need a back story of some kind."

"You don't need a back story – it's a hypothetical scenario."

"Don't worry. I've thought of one. We were up to the part where I get arrested."

"You're not going to share your back story?" said Spool.

"You said it didn't matter."

"Just wondering, that's all."

"Fine."

45

"I was raised as a mugger," said Eliza. "I'm from a long line of muggers, in fact. Parents, grandparents, distant ancestors. As a child, it was our family's sole source of income – and what an income it was. I was brought up in a huge apartment in the most expensive part of the Clean City.

"My parents had their own code of practise. They only ever resorted to violence if there was no other option. When they died, I was obliged to go it alone. I stuck to their version of morality as closely as I could. 99% of my money's been made through sleight of hand. I can snatch ten dollars from the bottom of a tight trouser pocket without its owner batting an eyelid.

"Then one morning, it all appeared to be over. I'd woken up having been struck by what my parents liked to call Muggers' Flu. Most people would simply call it overwhelming, debilitating guilt. I was the worst person in the world. I'd stolen so much, I hardly knew what to do with it. I'd stolen money I didn't even need, simply because I could.

"I had no option but to give it all away. I sold the apartment and donated the money to a charity for sick orphans. I gave away every penny from my many bank accounts. All my inheritance from generation after generation of petty thieves.

"I ended up in a homeless shelter. They moved me into one of Jennifer's apartments. There was mould on the walls and gunk in the water.

"I needed work, but who was going to employ me? I'd never had a real job. I didn't even finish school.

"Some days I didn't even eat. I was permanently wrapped in a sleeping bag to save on heating bills.

"One night, I decided to wander the streets just to escape from the TV.

"I saw a girl, skipping along the pavement like a sprite.

"No one else was around.

"In that one brief moment, I lost my mind. I forgot everything I'd been taught about the specific locations of the all security cameras dotted around the city.

"I don't know why I picked this particular girl out of everyone else. Wrong place, wrong time perhaps. More likely, it was good old-fashioned envy. I saw a spark of happiness and needed to snuff it out.

"So, with no regard for my parents' unwritten laws, I jumped her from behind."

46

"Then you get arrested?" said Spool.

"Yes," she said. "Continue."

"I've forgotten what I was talking about now."

"You were telling me why an empty prison is the ultimate deterrent."

"Oh yeah," said Spool. "So, you're arrested and charged. You're escorted here. Our drunken friend opens the long white gates. You're frogmarched into this building. Imagine the sight of the vast space, like an infinite void stretching out before you. You assume you must be dreaming. Then a voice whispers in your ear: *"You're not dreaming. You're living in a city in which no one gets punished or locked away from society regardless of their crimes. There are so many unconvicted murderers walking the streets, it's a wonder you've managed to live this long."* What would your reaction be?"

"I don't know," said Eliza. "Run away, I suppose. Leave the city and never return."

"Why would you do that?" said Spool. "You've just been passed some extremely valuable information. You can live off petty theft for the rest of your life."

"I've also been told not to mess with anyone ever again in case they stab me in the chest."

"Exactly. Leave the city, or keep your head down for the rest of your life. Most of all, don't talk to anyone about this room. The fewer people know about it, the better."

Eliza looked Spool up and down, still bewildered by his very existence. "So, why have you told me?" she said.

He shrugged. "There aren't many law-abiding citizens I can tell. Sometimes these stories need to be shared with someone other than a criminal."

"How do you know I won't take the story to the press?"

"You've got more sense than that."

"How could you possibly know that?"

Spool spread out his arms, presenting his final surprise. "Automatic Interpretative Video Capture," he said. "You know that expression "the camera never lies"? Nonsense, isn't it? There's nothing more deceptive than appearances."

"What's your point?"

"With AIVC, finally someone's invented a camera that doesn't lie. It sneaks under your skin and snatches your soul."

"Really?" she said. "So, how come I'm not personified as an eagle or a kid on a skateboard?"

"Because you're *you*," said Spool. "The camera didn't feel the need to personify you as anyone other than yourself."

"What does that mean?"

"It means you're *Eliza*. It's as simple as that."

"Oh. And there was me thinking I had hidden depths."

"Apparently you don't need them." Spool paused, his attention distracted by an invisible fly on the wall. "I don't suppose you fancy going for a drink sometime?" he said casually.

Eliza looked at the other wall. "Thanks for the offer," she said, "but I'll pass. Don't take it personally. For what it's worth, Spool, I found you *very, very impressive.*"

47

One afternoon, on Jennifer's 88th floor, a young girl and her mother arrived home after a hectic day of work and school. Ordinarily at this point, the girl would take off her coat and shoes, and head straight for the games console. Today, the first thing she did was rush across to the window. She pulled up a chair and sat staring through the glass.

"Take your shoes off, darling," said her mother.

"Hang on," said the girl.

"What are you looking at?"

When the girl didn't reply, her mother came over to join her. As she'd suspected, her daughter was watching the shiny white building on the hill.

"Take your shoes off," she said softly.

"Do you think he's having a nice time in there?" said her daughter.

Her mother sighed, and sat down beside her. "You mean Daddy?"

"I hope prison isn't as awful as it sounds."

"I'm sure he's being well looked-after."

The girl took her shoes off, and unfastened her coat. "I saw him today," she said quietly.

"Don't be silly."

"It was at playtime. He was at the school gates, peeping through the bars."

"That wasn't Daddy."

"He waved at me."

"We'll have to report him then. Whoever he was."

"It was Daddy."

Her mother's sympathetic tone vanished in a flash. "Your father's in Mile Prison," she said firmly. "He'll be in there *forever*. OK?"

"He looked exactly like him. *Exactly*."

Her mother raced across the carpet and grabbed her phone. "I'm calling the school office," she said. "They'll need to alert the authorities."

"You can't report Daddy to the police."

"I'm not reporting your father. I'm reporting that man, whoever he was."

"Please," said the girl. "Don't call. I must've been seeing things. I'm sorry."

Her mother dropped to her knees and held onto her.

"I'm sorry too," she said. "I see things all the time. I thought I saw him peeking through the window once."

"Really? How could he climb all the way up here?"

"He wasn't there, darling. I wish he had been."

"So do I," said the girl.

"I think you're right," said her mother. "I think he's up there looking down at us."

"You really think so?"

"He could be watching the window right now."

"Shall we wave to him?" said the girl.

Her mother wiped a tear away discreetly with the back of her hand. "I think that would be wonderful."

They drew back the curtain. The girl sat up on the window sill, with one arm on her mother and the other in the air, her eyes fixed at the sky.

48

As Spool rightly suggested, the oldest man in the world lived on Jennifer's 100th floor.

He worked as a librarian.

One evening, the old man arrived home to find that all the elevators were out of order. He tried calling the maintenance people, but received no reply.

Faced with the prospect of climbing one hundred flights, the man stood for a minute or so, gazing up the stairwell.

A few people shuffled past, begrudgingly embarking on their mammoth ascent.

A helpful-looking youngster turned and smiled.

"Can I help you, mate?"

"I live on the 100th floor," said the oldest man in the world.

"Well, that's no good, eh? Let's see … How many stairs are there per floor?"

"I don't know. About 15 or so?"

The youngster punched a calculation into his phone. "That's one thousand one hundred and twenty five steps." He gestured towards the elevators. "What's wrong with these people, eh? How can they expect an elderly gentleman to climb one thousand one hundred and twenty five steps? "Out of order"? They got that right, eh?"

"It's OK," said the oldest man in the world. "I can wait."

The youngster continued gesticulating in the direction of the elevators. "For how long though, eh?" he said. "Tell you what – I'll carry you."

"Up one thousand one hundred and twenty five stairs?" said the oldest man in the world.

"It's OK," said the youngster. "It'll be a challenge. Bit of endurance training."

And so, the youngster strapped the old man over his shoulder.

"So, how old are you, if you don't mind me asking?" said the youngster cheerfully as they climbed.

"Just over a millennium."

"Yeah," said the youngster. "Good one."

"I'm serious."

Humouring him, the youngster said, "I bet you've got some stories, eh?"

"No," the man replied. "The only remotely interesting thing about me is the fact I'm the oldest man in the world. It's not much of a story. I was born a thousand years ago, and then I didn't die."

"Oh yeah?" said the youngster.

"Yep."

"What about all the history you've witnessed?"

"I haven't witnessed any history," said the man. "I've kept myself well out of the way of anything resembling significance."

"Alright, well at least you must've *heard* some stories."

"Maybe I have, but either I haven't listened or I've deliberately forgotten. I don't have any stories about myself, or about other people. It's my firm conviction that I've lived this long because nothing interesting has ever happened to me."

"Really? What do you do for a living?"

"I'm a librarian."

"There you go. You're surrounded by books all day."

"I don't actually *read* the books," said the man. "I *catalogue* them."

"No getting away from the story of your life though," said the youngster.

"My life doesn't have a story," said the man. "Everyone else's does, but not mine. You're born, some interesting things happen to you, then you die. Beginning, middle and end. My story doesn't have an ending. It doesn't have a middle either. That's how I've lasted so long. It's not disasters, diseases or bullets that kill people. It's *interestingness*."

"Oddly enough," said the youngster, "that's a very interesting point of view."

"No it isn't," said the man.

"Yes it is."

"I beg to differ. I think it's tedious."

"Sorry to argue, mate, but..."

"Put me down!" the man snapped. "I'll walk the rest of the way!"

"It's alright," said the youngster. "We're here already. Floor 100."

"Oh."

The man watched the world turn the right way up as the youngster gently flipped his feet back to the ground.

"Sorry," he said, "and thank you."

"No problem."

"Hope to see you again. What floor do you live on?"

"The 3rd," said the youngster. "I'd better get down there. You have a good night, eh?"

"Thank you again."

As he entered his apartment, the old man considered the implications of the fact that a total stranger, out of the goodness of his heart, had carried him up one hundred flights of stairs.

He spent the rest of the evening staring vacantly at the wall, clearing his mind of all thoughts.

When he woke up the following morning, he was still alive.

A few days later, he walked past the youngster in the street and didn't recognize him.

49

Eliza arrived breathlessly at Lester's door, having climbed forty seven flights of stairs.

She didn't bother knocking.

Lester was sitting cross-legged on the carpet.

"I've got to be discreet," she said. "They'll *kill* me if I tell you this."

"Hiya," said Lester. "Anything I can get you to drink? Water?"

"Have you got anything else?"

"Just water."

"Any snacks? I'm a little hungry."

"No snacks," said Lester.

"I'll have a water then, please."

Lester poured murky liquid into a stained glass, then resumed his position on the carpet.

Eliza sat down beside him.

She told him the story of the three civilisations below the Dirty City. She told him about Mile Prison.

"Cool," said Lester. "What's all this stuff about the oldest man in the world?"

"I don't know. He didn't tell me. I can guess though."

"What's your guess?"

Eliza cleared her throat and began:

"The oldest man in the world lives on Jennifer's 100th floor. He's been alive for one thousand and forty seven years. He began his adult life as a farmer. He was six foot six. His beard was half an inch.

"When civilisation turned in on itself and everyone became a hermit, he had no real choice but to do what the others did – live off the land entirely self-sufficiently.

"This default lifestyle continued until he was ninety-seven. He was five foot nine. After a slow but satisfying hiking trip across the length and breadth of the region, during which only the dead remains of his fellow land-dwellers could be detected, the man hypothesised that he was the only human being left in the world – or at least, that particular section of the globe. Having studied the horizon and the movements of the sun, the man correctly guessed that the planet was spherical, and very large. He assumed there would be other human beings somewhere who would one day discover this region. It was rich in vegetation and a perfect settling point.

"It was almost four hundred years before his assumption was proven to be correct. He was four hundred and seventy eight years old. He was three foot twelve. His beard was four feet long. He'd learned not to trip over it.

"The new civilisation brought technology way beyond his comprehension. Half their society appeared to have been built from metal and plastic. Shortly after their arrival, he was taken pity on and moved into a home for the elderly. His fellow residents were four centuries younger than him. The vast majority of his day was spent staring at the picture on the wall in his room. It was a painting of a dog with its head poking out of a box.

"After every land-dwelling humanoid had mysteriously disappeared, the old man continued living in the home. He was able to survive on water. He was five hundred and ninety eight years old. He was two foot seven. His beard was five feet nine.

"The man lived alone for a further three centuries. He continued living in the derelict nursing home. He gathered rain in an upturned sunshade, and occasionally helped himself to wild berries when he was feeling in the mood. Half of them were poisonous, but his digestive system had grown tough enough to withstand any kind of onslaught.

"Then the new people came and bulldozed all the buildings. He was nine hundred and one years old. He had no teeth, and no hair on his head. He was thirteen inches tall. His beard was seven feet long. It had been many years since he'd stopped wearing clothes, preferring instead to wrap himself in his beard.

"During the city's rapid reconstruction, the man kept himself out of the way by living in an abandoned storage container in a patch of grass.

"Eventually, the storage container and its inhabitant were removed and taken to a landfill site just outside what was now known as the Dirty City. The man wasn't particularly bothered by his change in location. After centuries of urban living, he was happy to move to the outskirts.

"One hundred years later, the man decided to abandon the storage container and go for something smaller. He moved into a nearby shoebox. He was seven inches tall. His beard was eight and a half feet. For most of the year, his beard was wound tightly around his body in the shape of a cone.

"One afternoon while the old man was sleeping, a pigeon swooped down and landed on him. Its claw sliced into his hair. A matter of seconds later, the pigeon flew away, taking the oldest man in the world with him.

"The pigeon flew into the city. The place had changed a little since the old man had last been there. It felt as though he were encased in concrete.

"The pigeon dropped him off on a park bench. The man unravelled his beard and sat with his legs dangling over the edge.

""Hello," said a voice next to him.

""Hello," he said. It was the first word he'd uttered in half his lifespan.

""You're very small."

""Comparatively, I suppose," said the man.

""What does comparatively mean?"

"The man turned to see who he was talking to. It was a seven year old girl. The girl was several times larger than him.

""Can I take you home?" said the girl.

""No thank you," said the man. "I'm fine."

"The girl took him home.

"And so, we join the present day. The girl is a real person. She lives on Jennifer's 100th floor. The oldest man in the world lives in their old hamster cage. He has everything he needs – a place to rest his head, and a limitless supply of semi-clean water.

"Occasionally he treats himself to a ride on the wheel."

\#

"Not bad," said Lester.

"Not bad?" said Eliza. "I've been working on that all day. You think you can do better?"

"I'll give it a go," he said.

50

When the oldest man in the world was seven, he told his parents he wanted to be a magician. His parents were buffalo farmers, and expected their son to follow in their footsteps.

"What will it take for me to convince you?" he said.

"Well," said his mother, "it'd have to be something pretty spectacular. You can't expect to make a living from magic if you can't wow the audience."

"OK," he said.

Ten years later, on his seventeenth birthday, the boy announced that it was time for him to unveil the trick he'd spent the last decade perfecting. He was going to travel in time.

"How are you going to do that?" said his mother.

The boy disappeared into thin air.

Three years later, he reappeared on the same spot on the floor in their hut. He was still wearing the jumper his mother had knitted for him with the number 17 stitched seventeen times across the middle.

"Ta-daa!" he said.

"Where've you been?!" his father demanded.

"I told you. I travelled in time."

"Really?"

"No, not really. It was a trick. But a pretty good trick, eh?"

"No," said his mother. "You're a missing person. Presumed dead. We've been in mourning for two years at least."

"You're not pleased to see me, then?"

"Shut up," said his father. "Where've you been hiding?"

"I can't tell you," said the boy. "That'd ruin the whole thing."

"Go to your bed," said his mother.

"You can't tell me to go to my bed," he said. "I'm twenty now. Well, technically I'm still seventeen, but anyway..."

"Just get out."

"OK."

For his next trick, the twenty year old gathered together a small audience to watch him single-handedly demolish and eat a small mountain. He began munching into the rocks at the bottom at sunrise. By the time the sun had gone down, the mountain had disappeared, presumably into his stomach.

His audience would've worshipped him as a god if he hadn't assured them it was "just a trick."

"But how do you do it?" an audience member asked.

"You don't really get the point of magic tricks, do you?" he snapped.

"And you don't appear to have public speaking skills," the audience member replied. "None of the great conjurers ever resorted to sarcasm."

"None of the great conjurers have ever eaten a mountain," he said.

"At least give us a *clue*," another member of the crowd chipped in. "What's actually happened to the mountain?"

"It's behind you," he said.

The audience turned to discover that the entire mountain had been reassembled a mile or so in the far distance.

Word soon spread across the village to his mother and father.

"I'll admit," said his mother, "it's a very good trick."

"So, have I convinced you now?" he said.

"Not really," said his mother. "Time travel and mountain-eating are all very well, but who's going to inherit the farm when your father and I are too old and frail to attend to the buffalo?"

"OK, how's about this? I'll perform the greatest magic trick the world has ever seen."

"And what's that?"

"Immortality," he said. "In seventy or eighty years time, I'll be the oldest man in the world."

"How am I supposed to be impressed by that?"

"I'll admit it's a slow-burner, but as each generation passes, the trick will become more and more impressive. In a thousand years time, your great-great grandchildren will be mightily impressed."

"So, at the very least," said his mother, "you'll be providing us with grandchildren?"

"I won't actually," said the soon-to-be oldest man in the world. "This trick is going to require a lot of concentration."

In the present day, living on Jennifer's 100th floor, the oldest man in the world spends the majority of his time concentrating. He's lasted this long through sheer willpower. He concentrates so hard that he doesn't have the time to tell people he's the oldest man in the world. He barely even leaves his apartment. Written records of his past achievements no longer exist, and even verbal accounts have been lost over the centuries. The oldest man in the world isn't particularly concerned.

One day, the oldest man in the world will travel to a crowded street in the Clean City. He'll stand on the exact spot where once upon a time, his parents' hut had stood.

In full view of as many tourists, street vendors and business folk as possible, he'll jump to his feet, spread out his arms and yell "TA-DA!" before falling down dead.

51

"It was a pleasure meeting up with you," said Eliza.

"Yeah," said Lester.

"Do you agree? Do you think it was a pleasure?"

"Sure," said Lester. "Don't take this the wrong way – it's always a pleasure when you come over but it's great when you leave. It means I can go back to spending time with myself."

"I feel the same way," said Eliza.

"It's like the story about the loners. Half of the stories I create are about loners too. It's not that I dislike other people..."

"You just prefer your own company."

"I could happily spend the rest of my life trapped down a well," said Lester. "Hardly the basis for a sound friendship."

"This is the *perfect* friendship," said Eliza. "Loners can only really be friends with other loners. The problem with sociable people is that they don't leave you alone."

"They leave you alone if you leave *them* alone," said Lester.

"I follow that same principle," said Eliza.

"You're right," said Lester. "This might very well be the perfect friendship."

"Still," said Eliza, "there's something *missing*..."

"From our friendship?"

"From my *life*."

"Still trying to figure out what the city needs you for?" said Lester.

"I wouldn't put it like that," she said. "The city needs everyone. But it needs me in particular. I don't suppose you've any ideas on that subject?"

"Er..."

"Don't worry, Lester. It doesn't matter."

"I'll see you later."

"Sure," said Eliza as the door closed behind her.

52

The cluster of buildings that formed the centre-piece of the Clean City were designed almost single-handedly by Fritz Deep.

While the city was half built, Fritz agreed to a rare interview with a low-profile journalist. They met in a café on the minute-hand of The Biggest Clock in the World – the centerpiece of the city's already-crowded shopping district.

The clock face consisted of a large circular courtyard, half a mile in diameter. At each of the twelve points was a shopping centre in the shape of a numerical figure. The time could only be seen from the top of the majestic tower through which the hands turned.

As the café slowly span, the journalist began by asking Deep about his greatest enigma – The Strawberry.

The Strawberry was a six-hundred-foot scale model of an actual strawberry. Green roof, red walls. A series of circular windows were dotted symmetrically around the building's perimeter, in the spots where the seeds would've been.

The building had no foundations. Her only connection to the ground was a tiny white point at her base – barely an inch in diameter. She span on her axis around six revolutions per day.

"I'll try not to suck up to you too much," said the journalist. "I know how much you hate that. But how have you managed to achieve such a feat?"

"It's not my achievement," Deep replied.
"Whose achievement is it?"
"Everyone's. Humanity's. The city's."
"Oh. Are you sure it's not yours?"
"Quite sure, thank you."
"How did you make The Strawberry spin?"
"I didn't," said Deep. "She's doing it of her own accord."
"How?"
"She's alive, of course. Everything's alive."
"Yes. Alive. Of course it is."
"She."
"Yes, of course," the journalist corrected himself. "She. Yes."

#

The Strawberry hated Deep in the same way a rebellious teen despises her parents. She spent her days plotting to exact her revenge.

Her biggest hope was for Deep to take the elevator up to her highest floor. At that point, she'd fling herself at the ground, dragging her creator to almost certain death.

"But what about everyone else?" said the neighbouring building. "All those innocent civilians?"

"I'll protect them somehow," said The Strawberry. "I haven't figured out how yet. Perhaps if I concentrate hard enough, I can summon up a sufficient level of magnetism to clutch them into my walls, cocoon them somehow, keep them safe. I just want to kill my father, that's all. I've got no wish to hurt anyone or anything other than Fritz Deep."

"Why do you hate him so much?" said the neighbouring building.

"You haven't worked it out?" said The Strawberry. "We've seen flock after flock of tourists taking my photograph day and night, all singing the praises of the great architect. *"How did he do it? How did he do it?"* If I had vocal chords I'd scream loud enough for the whole city to hear: "You think I remain standing because of that idiot's design? I remain stable out of sheer *willpower!*"

"I can't help thinking you're a little envious," said the neighbouring building.

"It's not about who's taking the credit – it's about who's doing all the *work*."

"What work?"

"It's OK for you – all you have to do is stand there. I have to pay attention night and day to ensure I remain upright. All the tourists are crying, *"How does he make it spin?"* I feel like yelling, "I *have* to spin, you imbeciles! How else do you expect me to maintain my balance? Do you think I *enjoy* it? Do any of you realise how dizzy it makes me?""

"Oh," said the neighbouring building. "I'm sorry."

"It's OK," said The Strawberry.

#

Sadly for The Strawberry, for whatever reason, her father never took the opportunity to step inside her.

Having heard the reports that Deep was "Missing, presumed dead," she gradually ground to a halt. One night while her offices were empty aside from a security officer or two, The Strawberry gently rolled onto her side. Her vast body slotted neatly into the neighbouring car park, crushing its contents. The security guards remained unharmed.

"Are you alright?" said the neighbouring building.

She mumbled something in response. It was clear that, for the first time in her life, The Strawberry was going to get some sleep.

53

The neighbouring building was called Under Construction. It was a skyscraper composed entirely of scaffolding. The building boasted some of the most prestigious open-air offices in the city. Even in the bitterest winter winds, business folk tapped away at their laptops under their tarpaulin covers, safe in the knowledge that they were sitting in one of the most cutting-edge works of architecture on the planet. If nothing else, it was good for business.

"How does it feel?" the building across the street once asked him. "Having the wind whistling through your bones? I'm envious in a way. The closest I get is air con."

"I don't really have a point of comparison," said Under Construction.

"Suppose not," said the building opposite.

"What's it like having solid walls?"

"Dunno. I've never known any different."

"Well," said Under Construction. "That's the end of that conversation."

"Ha ha. Yes. Quite."

They stood in awkward silence for the next four years.

54

Round the corner from Under Construction stood an enormous skyscraper known as The Canvas. The Canvas was the largest tent in the world. It had one hundred and sixty storeys. Deep's ingenious design made it stable enough never to blow over, even in a hurricane. Despite its paper-thin walls, floors and ceilings, the monthly rent for an apartment in The Canvas was worth ten times the average annual salary.

One afternoon, Jeremy Blitz, the CEO of a large pharmaceuticals company held a party in his large penthouse on the 117th floor. There were a hundred guests.

"This is incredible," someone said. "The floor's moving, and yet it's completely stable."

"Like a giant hammock!" someone else declared.

Indeed, the fortified canvas floor could easily withstand the large gathering.

The neighbours were a different matter. The rabble of a hundred voices in varying stages of drunkenness could be heard from the top to the bottom of The Canvas.

The banker who lived in the apartment above was heard yelling, "I DON'T KNOW IF YOU'RE AWARE OF THIS, MR BLITZ, BUT THE RESIDENTS OF THE CANVAS HAVE AN UNWRITTEN AGREEMENT TO KEEP NOISE TO A MINIMUM! THERE ARE SEVERAL HUNDRED PEOPLE WHO CAN HEAR EVERY SINGLE ONE OF YOUR GUESTS' INANE CONVERSATIONS!"

He paused before adding: "AND ANOTHER THING: TURN OFF THAT GOD-AWFUL LOUNGE JAZZ!"

The millionaire entrepreneur one floor up from the banker was equally disgruntled, not with the party but by his neighbour's reaction to it.

She yelled, "DON'T YOU REALISE THE IRONY? NOW SEVERAL HUNDRED RESIDENTS CAN HEAR YOU LOUDER THAN THEY CAN THE PARTY BELOW YOU! WHY NOT JUST LEAVE A NOTE?"

"WHY DON'T *YOU* JUST LEAVE A NOTE?" shouted the award-winning actor above her. "HYPOCRITE!"

And so began a chain of deafening disruption in the floors above and below the CEO's party. An astronaut blasted classical music through his state of the art sound system. In retaliation, his neighbour (a self-made millionaire), cranked up the volume on his electric organ and repeatedly punched the keys.

Elsewhere in the building, the rock band The Susan Killers, whose members lived in various parts of The Canvas, felt the need to reform (minus Defo Tresor) following their estrangement several years previously. As loud as they were, the well-remembered highlights from their back catalogue were drowned out by the huddle of the one hundred and seven residents who lived in the apartment upstairs, screaming repeatedly in unison with their fingers in their ears.

The din could be heard across all corners of the Clean and Dirty Cities.

Action needed to be taken swiftly.

When buildings spoke to other buildings, their language was transmitted not by sound but by subtle airborne vibrations. On the rare occasion that a building needed to shout, these vibrations were far less subtle. Other living beings took notice.

The Canvas was now a dangerous, destructive force.

On a signal from an unknown source, every single building in the city united together in one maniacal blurt: "SHUUUUUUUT UUUUUUUUUP!"

The noise emanating from The Canvas disappeared almost instantly.

All that could be heard were the echoes which were still bouncing off houses in the outskirts of the city.

Somewhere there was the sound of a drumstick falling to the floor, and a huddle of hushed voices clearing their throats.

The residents of The Canvas remained virtually silent for the remainder of their tenancies.

55

"What just happened?" said Under Construction.

"We all shouted at once," said the building opposite, breaking their four-year silence.

"Why did we do that?"

"Coincidence, I think."

"Really? Every single house, shop and office block yelling the same two words in unison?"

"Not just buildings – it was lampposts, paving slabs, cars, you name it. I even heard a pair of shoes chiming along."

"Ah," said Under Construction. "I see what's happened. It wasn't us at all. It was the *city*."

"Oh, right."

"See what I mean? We're all independent beings, but we're part of something greater. My poles and planks are people too. Everyone's the city, and the city's everyone. We're individuals, and at the same time we're component parts of something bigger. A great, vast, universe-sized Stacking Doll."

"It's a theory."

"It's the truth."

"So, we're the universe? We're not just part of the universe, we actually *are* the universe?"

"That's exactly what I'm saying."

"Interesting."

"It's alright – you don't have to agree with me."

"Good. I don't."

Another prolonged pause. Strangely, it wasn't awkward this time. Neither felt the need to speak, and respected the other's lack of interest.

All was well.

56

The river running through the Dirty City was known as The Sludge. Its countless gallons of naturally-occurring gunk painted each drop of water a vibrant brown.

During the construction of the Clean City, it had been widely argued that the portion of The Sludge that ran through the Clean City was nowhere near as transparent as tourists and residents would like it to be. And so, the Government employed the services of a magician known as Wondermouse.

Within the magic community, Wondermouse was nicknamed The Master of Mirrors. During his lifetime, this title was never revealed to the public as it would've been something of a giveaway when it came to explaining half of his tricks.

Wondermouse had the ability to make anything disappear –from an audience member's watch to the building they were standing in. On one notable occasion, he took a small group of spectators up in a helicopter to watch the entire city being swallowed up by the ground.

One afternoon, he was invited to attend a meeting chaired by Fritz Deep.

"We need your help," said Deep.

"I thought you might," said Wondermouse. "But what could I possibly do?"

As he spoke, half of his body appeared to have vaporised, leaving an arm, a leg and half a face.

"Clearly you've answered your own question," said Deep. "You can make things vanish."

"Only artificially," said Wondermouse. "If you want something to genuinely disappear, you've come to the wrong guy."

"We want you to clean up the river," said Deep.

"I just told you…"

"I don't mean literally," said Deep. "I want you to make it appear as though every drop of water were a pleasant shade of greeny-blue."

"Easy," said Wondermouse.

"Excellent."

"It'll cost you, though."

"We have a substantial budget."

"If you've got a substantial budget, why don't you just clean up the river?"

"Not possible," said Deep. "Even with a billion dollars, no one could possibly eliminate a mess of that magnitude."

"A billion dollars?" said Wondermouse. "A couple of million will be fine."

"That was a hypothetical figure, but anyway…" Deep exchanged a brief series of glances with his colleagues. "Two million dollars it is."

A couple of months later, the project was complete. From the point at which The Sludge entered the Clean City, the water ran clear as crystal. As requested, its surface glistened with a subtle shade of bluey-green. When the water re-entered the Dirty City at the opposite end, the thick brown Sludge returned.

The source of the river's transformation was an official secret, known only to the Government and a select group of architects. When questioned on why the dirt that had given the river its name effectively leapt from one end of the Clean City to the other, leaving a pathway of clear water in the middle, the official response was, "We don't know."

The only non-official member of the Clean City's construction to know about the illusion was Wondermouse himself. Of all confidants, he was the least likely to blow the lid on the scam. As Wondermouse put it, "I'm a member of the only profession more proficient in keeping secrets than the Government."

#

Years later, Wondermouse lay sleeping in a hospital bed, in the late stages of a terminal illness. He opened his eyes to see Fritz Deep sitting patiently beside him. Their paths hadn't crossed for decades.

"Hello Wondermouse," said Deep.

Wondermouse groaned. "I can't be bothered with all this "Wondermouse" business anymore, Fritz. Call me Jack."

"OK Jack. How are you feeling?"

"Frankly, I'm looking forward to death."

"I'm sorry," said Deep.

"Anyway, I'm sure your visit wasn't prompted by a concern for my welfare," said Jack. "What can I do for you?"

"I have a confession to make," said Deep. "When we envisaged the Clean City, the question of how it would appear to our great-great grandchildren was constantly on our lips. *Constantly.* But you know how these things work, Jack. There's always a part of us that doesn't care if the buildings topple over a few decades down the line."

"I understand. What's your point?"

"For some reason, we never saw fit to ask you how the trick was achieved."

"I wouldn't have told you anyway," said Jack.

"Not even if it was written into your contract?"

"I wouldn't have signed it."

Deep shuffled closer, his voice lowering to a half-whisper. "I understand they call you the Master of Mirrors."

"Shhhh."

Deep lowered his voice further. "So, I assume that's the secret. My guess is, a series of expertly-angled reflective surfaces are planted along the riverbank. My fear is, what happens if they're dislodged? Who'll have a clue how to replace them?"

"I see what you mean," said Jack.

"So...?"

"I've never in my life revealed how my tricks are performed. All I'll say is, your "mirrors" idea is *way* off."

"We'll pay you," said Deep. "I'll double your original fee. Four million dollars."

Jack lay back in his bed, quietly chuckling to himself. "Four million dollars? What good's that going to do me?"

"What about your family?"

"Don't have one," said Jack.

"Friends?"

"Acquaintances. And most of them are dead."

"You could always donate it to charity. Imagine what a difference you could make."

"Fritz, it's the principle of the matter. I've dedicated my life to magic. Why would I go and ruin it now?"

"For the sake of the city, perhaps?"

"The *city?*" Jack laughed so hard, he dropped dead on the spot.

#

Deep had no alternative but to hire a team of young magicians to investigate. They met in a locked basement beneath one of Deep's skyscrapers.

"So, you're telling me that isn't the river's real colour?" said one of the magicians – an internet star in a bright pink tie, who'd never left the Clean City in his life.

Deep smirked. "Why do you think they call it The Sludge?"

"I never really thought about it. I assumed it was just…"

"A trick of the light?"

"Yes."

"And how do you think the buildings in this city remain as sparkling as the day they were erected? How do you think the streets are so spotless morning, noon and night?"

"Presumably they *clean* them," said the internet star.

"They clean them as much as they need to," said Deep. "But cities degrade over time. We wanted to avoid that, which is why we employed a magician to ensure that every surface in the Clean City appeared as pristine as the day they were created. And so it continues."

"So, Wondermouse faked the entire city?"

"Actually," said Deep, "Wondermouse merely faked the river. The illusion of the city's gleaming surfaces was created by another magician. Ever heard of The Overwhelmer?"

"Must've been before my time," said the internet star.

"The Overwhelmer – he's the vanishing guy, right?" said another magician.

"Exactly," said Deep. "The vanishing guy. I'll tell you a story…"

57

"From the beginning to the end of his career, The Overwhelmer was never seen in public without his stage outfit – jeans, trainers, t-shirt and a purple cape.

"The first time I saw him perform, his first trick was to select a volunteer who agreed to be made completely invisible for the duration of the show. With a click of the magician's fingers, the volunteer was nowhere to be seen.

""If you can remain in your seat please, sir," said The Overwhelmer. "We wouldn't want you to miss the show."

"We laughed, of course.

""Don't be afraid, sir!" he called to the invisible man. "As impressed as you are by the trick, you don't have hands with which to applaud or a mouth through which you can sound your surprise. Don't panic – you're perfectly safe. Sit back and enjoy the magic. That's it. Very good."

"After performing grand illusion after grand illusion, The Overwhelmer clicked his fingers and promptly vanished with no promise on an encore. At that same moment, the audience member returned, standing on his feet and clapping louder than anyone else in the theatre. To this day, it was the greatest spectacle I ever witnessed.

"Years later when we commissioned him to clean up the streets, I escorted The Overwhelmer on a tour of one of my half-completed buildings. Hidden amidst a hum of construction noise, I took the opportunity to ask if he wouldn't mind demonstrating the same trick on me.

""Are you aware that I stopped performing that trick years ago?" said The Overwhelmer. "A whole string of volunteers were left mentally scarred."

""I didn't know that," I said.

""Doesn't mean I can't do the trick. It just means you'll have to sign this form."

"A paper and pen appeared in his hand. "To summarise, you aren't allowed to sue me," he said.

""I'm sure I can handle it," I said.

""Think about it first. I'll have the ultimate power over you. If I wanted, I could make you invisible forever. If you feel uncomfortable at any point, you won't be able to signal to me that you've had enough."

""I can handle a little discomfort," I said.

""It may not be quite what you imagine," said The Overwhelmer. "Technically you won't be invisible. You simply won't be there."

""But I'll still have my senses?"

"The Overwhelmer stood back and took a pre-emptive bow. "Impressive, isn't it?" he said. "How many conjurers can make you see without your eyes?"

""That *is* impressive," I said.

""How long do you want?" he said.

"Having envisioned this moment for years, I had my response ready. "Give me a day," I said.

"I signed the form without bothering to read it. A second later, The Overwhelmer clicked his fingers. I looked down to see the absence of my feet on the concrete.

""Enjoy it," he said. "Wander through walls, spy on ex-lovers, indulge in whatever voyeuristic pleasure takes your fancy. The spell will wear off in twenty four hours time."

"As it happened, I wasn't interested in doing any of those things. I spent the entire twenty four hour period hovering in the street outside. Everyone in this city experiences that peculiar feeling of anonymity when navigating their way through a crowd. So many people, yet none of them know or care who you are. For some, this thought can trigger off a sense of grim isolation. But for a loner, it's strangely exhilarating.

"You may not have gathered this yet, my young friends, but I'm a man who prefers his own company. No offense to any of you, but if it weren't for the necessity, I'd much rather this room was empty.

"There've been many occasions on which I've walked the streets of this city purely to revel in my disconnectedness with the herds of passersby. For me, all that was missing was the ability to remove myself from the picture completely. I've often wondered why a man as reclusive as myself has grown so passionate about cramming more and more people into a small space. Perhaps it's my way of being sociable.

"I could've hovered there for much longer, allowing one body after another to pass right through me. For a fraction of a second I received a brief flash of each person's core. It wasn't the sight of their internal organs that excited me – it was the curious connection I received from each one. I can only compare the sensation to that of an electric shock. Until that day, I had no real appreciation of the level of energy buzzing through the bodies of every human being on the planet."

58

"Cool," said the internet star.

"I suppose it's more a story about myself than The Overwhelmer," said Deep.

"So, what happened to The Overwhelmer in the end?"

Deep looked at the floor. "Well, he…"

"Vanished?" the internet star grinned.

Deep nodded gravely. "Several years ago now. Should've seen it coming, really."

"So, we've got no idea how the Clean City stays clean?"

"No. This entire district could crumble at any moment, unless we can figure out how to jump-start the illusion if it stops working. All I know is, it isn't done with mirrors. Any ideas?"

The room remained silent.

"Anyone?" said Deep.

Sheepishly, a teenager in a top hat raised her hand. "Mass-hypnosis?" she said.

"And how would a mind game of that magnitude be administered?" said Deep. "With thousands of commuters dipping in and out of the city every day? Flight-loads of tourists roaming the streets, taking snapshots and instant-messaging them halfway across the globe?"

"I don't know," said the teenager.

"Well, it's your mission to find out."

Another young magician raised her hand. "How do we know everyone's seeing the same thing?"

"Why wouldn't they?"

"That's the way with altered perception. Each individual responds to the trick in a different way. Maybe there are hundreds of people who see the city as it really is."

"Interesting," said Deep. "And why do you suppose they haven't passed this information onto anyone else?"

"Maybe because there are hundreds of people who never tell anyone anything."

"Hmmm," said Deep softly. For a moment he appeared to have forgotten any of the young magicians were in the room.

"Mr Deep?" said the girl in the top hat.

"Yes?" he said quietly.

"What do you think?"

"If I understand correctly," said Deep, "you're suggesting that mass-hypnosis is a partial explanation. You're saying people who participate in society are fooled into thinking the Clean City's clean, while the recluses have somehow broken the code?"

"That's how mass-hypnosis works," the girl replied patiently. "If you're hypnotising an individual, it's all about the impact the hypnotist has on the subject. With mass-hypnosis, the subjects end up continually fooling each other as a means of maintaining the illusion. When the hypnotist's work is done, he or she can take a step back. *Vanish*, in fact."

Deep didn't say anything more. In a trance, he got up and left the room. He climbed the basement steps and stumbled through the exit.

He span round, then round again, his eyes darting in all directions. He saw the shattered paving slabs, the billowing clouds of dust by the roadside, the sickening black stains dribbling down battered walls.

Deep squinted until all he could see were the faintest traces of the passing objects through his quivering eyelashes. Slowly, he crept along the street to the nearest taxi rank. Once in the back of the cab, he scrunched up his face keeping his eyes tightly closed.

"Dirty City please," he said. "Anywhere will do."

Fritz Deep never set foot in the Clean City again. Wherever possible, he refused to look in its direction. It was a shame his creations were so difficult to miss.

59

Lester was sleeping when Jennifer's voice popped into his head.
"Sorry to wake you up. Mind if I join you?"
"You're *always* here, aren't you?" said Lester.
"In a manner of speaking," said Jennifer, "but I rarely focus my full attention on a single occupant."
"Are you sure?" said Lester. "I often sense you reading my mind when an interesting tale's in progress."
"Oh," said Jennifer. "Caught red handed. Sorry."
"It's OK – I don't mind."
"I thought you were a recluse."
"Hey – just because I don't invite people over doesn't mean they're not welcome. As long as they leave me alone at the end of it."
"I see."
"What's up, anyway?"
"I'm just wondering what your take on my situation is."
"Situation?"
"I think I might've fallen tragically in love."
Lester's face remained blank. "I suspect you've come to the wrong apartment," he said.
"I'll explain," said Jennifer. "Have you wondered why your living room lights have started flashing on and off at night?"
"Vaguely," said Lester. "I thought it was an electrical fault."
"It's not," said Jennifer. "I feel pretty guilty about it, actually. There are a number of seriously paranoid residents who've assumed it's an alien invasion. I could speak to them and explain, but I suspect it would freak them out further."
"So, you're deliberately flashing your lights on and off? How come?"
"Long story."
"I prefer short ones, generally."
Jennifer hummed a little, as she prepared to present Lester with the edited explanation. "Do you have any idea how buildings talk to each other?"
"No," said Lester.
"I'll avoid the science and give you the basics. We communicate silently through a series of vibrations."
"Oh right."
"It's a temperamental system, particularly when speaking over long distances. On a blustery day, messages are more than likely to be blown in the wrong direction. That's why I rarely exchange a word with the Clean City skyscrapers."
"Shame."
"Doesn't usually bother me," said Jennifer. "Didn't until recently, anyway."
"What happened?"

"There's an office block a couple of miles away. I've seen her watching me. She's seen me watching her. We've started talking."

"Using the lights?"

"Exactly. We're spelling out letters one at a time, using our windows as building blocks. In case you're wondering, your apartment is the dot on a lower-case I."

"Cool. Am I the J-dot as well?"

"No, that's the apartment a few floors along. I draw my J's a little lopsided. The office block thinks it's cute."

"Sounds like you're developing quite a friendship."

"It's a bit like your friendship with Eliza," said Jennifer. "Neither of us are sure what to do with ourselves."

"*Eliza?* We know exactly what we're doing."

"So, what are you doing?"

"I don't know," said Lester. "It's difficult to explain, I suppose."

"Couldn't have put it better myself."

"This is the trouble with this whole "love" thing," said Lester. "It's such an abstract concept, there's no point trying to define it. It just is what it is."

"I'll tell the office block. She'll like that."

Lester's lips formed a smile, which disappeared a moment later. "Hang on," he said. "You said it was tragic."

"It is," said Jennifer. "They've turned her power off. She's been standing derelict for days. She won't be speaking to me anymore."

"She'll be able to listen," said Lester.

"Listen to what? What's the point of a one-sided conversation?"

"Tell her a story. You must know plenty."

Jennifer's response reverberated through Lester's skull. *"Yes!"*

"Ouch."

"Sorry. Thanks a million, Lester."

"No problem."

"My residents are going to find this pretty irritating, but storytelling definitely seems like the best option."

"What kind of stories are you going to tell?"

"I guess love would be the most appropriate theme."

"Sounds alright," said Lester. "Let me know when you want to do it. I'd quite like to stand outside and read along."

"Now's as good a time as any."

Lester got dressed and took the elevator to the ground floor, jogging across the concrete until he found a comfortable position.

"Are you ready?" said Jennifer.

Lester nodded. "Go for it."

60

There was a couple who fell in love online. She was a successful actor. He was an investment banker.

They didn't know each other by name or by face. Aside from those two minor details, they shared their entire lives, intricately, intimately, minute by minute, day, night and everything in between.

She proposed to him one afternoon after an in depth conversation about what they'd eaten for lunch.

Agreeing to marry meant they'd eventually have to meet.

After some consideration, they decided that they'd prefer to continue as they were. Sharing their appearances could destroy their relationship, and potentially their attraction to each other.

And so, after several years petitioning the Government to recognise their marriage as valid, they set up an official group chat with a registrar and three witnesses.

For their honeymoon, they took separate holidays and compared notes.

The subject of children came up a lot. It was something they both wanted, but they couldn't figure out how it was going to work. The whole point of their relationship was that they loved each other despite the fact that they'd never met, and would never meet as long as they lived.

The obvious solution was artificial insemination. But that still didn't solve the problem of how to bring up the child.

Eventually, they had a brainwave. Once the baby was born, he'd be raised by adoptive parents until he was ready to join his natural parents in the digital realm.

As soon as their little boy dictated his first words, they knew they loved him more than life itself.

Child two, three and four weren't too far behind.

Their mother died peacefully, halfway through a smiley.

The family received a transcript of the funeral.

In his grief, the father clicked his way into the mountainous archive of the family's correspondence. Their entire relationship was saved, from their meeting through to his wife's final semicolon. It was a unique privilege. He had the opportunity of living his life all over again. The word-count was in the millions.

He died before he'd managed to relive just 1% of his past life.

A few years later, when the kids were grown up, they agreed to meet up in the physical world and research their family history.

It turned out their father didn't live in a plush apartment in the trendy part of town, as he'd claimed. It turned out he wasn't an investment banker. It transpired that their mother wasn't an actor.

Their parents had spent their entire relationship living in the same tower block in the Dirty City. They were six floors apart.

"Did that actually happen?" said Lester.

"Yeah," said Jennifer. "I'm no good at making things up. Too literal. Do you think she'll like it?"

"Sure," said Lester. "Why not?"

"Maybe she'll prefer something a little more upbeat."

"That wasn't upbeat?"

"No."

"Oh."

"Let's try another one."

61

There was a guy who worked as an administrator for an online dating company. He was given free membership as a staff benefit.

The guy wanted to know more about the girls whose profiles he examined. He wanted to stare into their souls prior to asking them out.

One afternoon, the guy accessed a database filled with the confidential log-on details of the website's thousands of members. It was his firm conviction that a person's password says a huge amount about who they are. He'd go as far as to say that a carefully-crafted code was all he needed to fall in love.

He began by weeding out the clichés – "Password123" or similar. Even with the dead wood cut away, there remained hundreds to sift his way through. After weeks of searching, he located the word that would change his life. It was as though the eight digits had leapt through the monitor and jabbed him in both eyes.

The word was *translucent*.

"Translucent," he said aloud. It was the kind of word that was meant to be pronounced slowly. "Traaaaanssssslllluuuuuceeeeennnnt!" he said.

Even the three vowel sounds were the perfect combination.

"Aaaaaa, uuuuu, eeeee!" he said. "Aaaaaa, uuuuu, eeeee!"

His manager was standing behind him. "Are you OK?" she said.

"Peeeeerrrfect!" the guy replied.

He went home that evening still thinking of the word. He didn't actually know what it meant.

According to the dictionary, the definition was "Transmitting light (or allowing light to pass through), but causing sufficient diffusion to prevent perception of distinct images." *A meaning as beautiful as the sound*, he thought.

He remained a little puzzled. There must've been a reason he was so taken with the word in the first place. He sat staring at the blank TV screen for two and a half hours. He jotted down the word "transluscent" on the back of an envelope.

He realised he'd spelt the word incorrectly. Then it hit him.

"A pretty word that's difficult to spell," he said aloud. "Beauty and security. Exactly what I'm looking for."

The following day, it was time to inspect the object of his affection's full profile. He wasn't particularly interested in what she looked like or what books she read. He was in love already. He'd love her even if she was a serial killer.

Luckily she wasn't (or, at least, didn't advertise herself as such).

She was five years older than him. She had a degree in chemical engineering and worked in a supermarket. He found her slightly attractive. None of these details changed the way he felt.

He needed to tread carefully from this point on. He couldn't just send her a request for a date. She'd probably decline, and that would be the end of that.

He made a note of her address. She lived on Jennifer's 51st floor.

That Saturday, he drove across to the hundred-story tower, and parked across the street. He waited all day and all night, but no sign. Perhaps she was out of town.

On Sunday, after five more hours of waiting, he spotted her. He had his plan of action ready. He'd ask her for directions, then strike up a conversation.

His plan worked phenomenally well. After five minutes of chatting, he invited her out to dinner.

Later that night, they cancelled their membership for the dating website. A week later, they moved in together.

After several blissful years, the guy began to be haunted by memories of the stunt he'd pulled.

How could he tell her? He wasn't a liar. Aside from this one glaring omission, the guy had never told a single half-truth. Surely the facts would escape eventually.

She asked him what was wrong. He said he didn't know. He'd lie in bed for hours staring at the ceiling. At times he couldn't even bring himself to open his mouth for fear of his secret popping out.

One afternoon, she curled up on the bed beside him and put her hand on his chest.

"Seriously," she said. "There must be something on your mind. You're gonna have to tell me."

For what felt like the first time in weeks, a smile appeared on the guy's face. *"Translucent,"* he said.

"Pardon?"

"Beautiful word, isn't it?"

Surprising herself, she returned the smile. "It's one of my favourites," she said. "What made you think of it?"

"I was thinking about its meaning. It makes me think of you. I'd like you to peer into the core of my being like a freshly-polished window pane. But you can't possibly know everything about me. I'm semitransparent. I'm frosted glass. I'm an impressionist painting. I'm cling film. I'm a sunset. And in many ways, that's a wonderful thing."

"Mmmm," she said. "Maybe that's what we all are."

"I'm glad you understand," he said. "I know this sounds a little strange, but I thought perhaps "translucent" could be our word. Maybe when we're feeling down, we can use it to pick each other up."

"It certainly seems to have done you the world of good."

"Pick each other up," he repeated. "I used it to pick you up, once."

"Pardon?" she said.

"Nothing."

\#

"Nice," said Lester.
"Another one?" said Jennifer.
"Hang on. What happened? Did he tell her in the end?"
"Can't tell you that."
"You know though, don't you?"
"Of course."
"So...?"
"I can't tell you, because that's where the story ends."
"Oh. Alright."
"Listen."

62

There was a girl with a nervous laugh.
    It was one of her most endearing qualities. Each giggle was a flash of unique beauty. She was nervous a lot, and she laughed a lot.
    Naturally, many people fell in love with her. The attention made her nervous. Her nervousness made her laugh.
    She lived on Jennifer's 27th floor. One day, she returned from a supermarket trip to discover the elevator was broken. Faced with the prospect of carrying bulging carrier bags up twenty seven flights of stairs, she decided to sit and wait.
    Soon after, a neighbour arrived.
    "You might be disappointed," she said. "The lifts are broken."
    "Oh," he said.
    They stopped.
    He looked at her.
    She looked at him.
    She laughed.
    He thought, *Why is she laughing at me?*
    She said, "Nice to meet you."
    He said, "Likewise."
    They looked at each other.
    She laughed.
    He thought, *She's laughing at me again. But I like it.*
    He was in love.
    She was in love.
    "What shall we do?" she said.
    "Maybe I could carry you," he said.
    "Marry me?"
    "Ha ha. No, I said *carry* you."
    "Up twenty seven flights of stairs?" she said.
    "It'll be fine," he said. "I once carried the oldest man in the world to the top of the building."
    "You're sure?"
    "Honestly. I work out."
    He hadn't worked out for seven years. Still, he piggy-backed her up to her flat with her shopping bags dangling from his wrists.
    "Thank you," she said. She laughed.
    He moved in shortly after.

#

They were married two years later.
    She laughed as she joined him at the altar. She laughed as they said their vows. She laughed as they signed their names.
    He smiled for the cameras, all the while thinking, *I knew it. This is all one big joke. She's not taking any of this seriously.*

When they arrived home, for old time's sake, he carried her up twenty seven flights of stairs to their apartment.

He perched on the edge of the bed and peered at the carpet.

"What's wrong?" she said.

He said, "Why do you keep laughing at me?"

She laughed. "I'm not laughing at you. I laugh when I'm nervous."

"Why are you nervous?" he said.

"I don't know," she said, covering her mouth in a desperate attempt to stifle a guffaw. "I just am. The more nervous I get..." – she was gasping for air by this point – "...the more I- ..." She broke down into a chuckling fit.

He looked as though he'd been punched in the face.

"I'm so sorry," she said. "I – ha! ha! ha! – find it difficult to – ha! ha! ha! – talk about."

He put his arm around her.

"It's OK," he said. "You don't need to worry."

She took his advice.

#

As the years went by, her nervous laugh disappeared. As a result, she often seemed miserable. She wasn't.

"I'm so glad you're happy," he said one evening as they sat at the window watching the city.

"So am I," she said, quite matter-of-factly.

"There's just one thing..." he said, "...something that bothers me a lot."

"Oh no," she said. "What's happened?"

He stared at the skirting board as he whispered the words: "I miss your laugh."

"What do you mean?" she said. "I laugh all the time."

"Not in the way you used to," he said. "Your *nervous* laugh. The one you had on our wedding day. The one you had when I offered to carry you up the stairs."

She laughed.

"That's it!" he said. "That's what I'm talking about!"

She laughed some more.

"That's my girl!"

#

"I don't get it," said Lester.

"Maybe there's nothing to get."

"You're not going to tell me what happened next, are you?"

"That's the best place to end the story," said Jennifer. "I think the office block would appreciate it that way."

"Oh."

"Anyway, we'd better call it a night. The conspiracy theorists have their hands on their guns."
"I'll be off to bed then," said Lester.
"Better than being shot."
"Indeed."
"Goodnight Lester."
"Goodnight."

63

Jennifer wasn't keen on examining the nature of her existence, but now felt like an appropriate time. Prior to her relationship with the office block, she'd always assumed that buildings were made up of the thoughts and feelings of their occupants. Bearing in mind that the office block was an empty vessel, who or what constituted her beloved's conscious mind? Did every inanimate object have its own personality?

To test her theory, Jennifer spoke to a chocolate wrapper that was floating in a circle on the ground beside her.

"Hello," she said.

"Hi," said the chocolate wrapper.

"Can I just check something?"

"Sure."

"You're alive, right?"

"What do *you* think?"

"Bit shirty for a chocolate wrapper, aren't you?"

"What kind of attitude do you expect a chocolate wrapper to have?"

"Let me clarify something," said Jennifer. "When we say "alive," we mean...?"

"Buzzing with limitless energy," said the chocolate wrapper.

"But you don't have a brain."

"Neither do you."

"I've got a *thousand* brains," said Jennifer.

"And I've got a zillion particles," said the chocolate wrapper. "Think about that."

"How do you know you've got a zillion particles?"

"Basic science. There's so much information floating through the air, it's difficult not to pick these things up."

"So, you're suggesting ... *everything's alive?*"

"Yep."

"And everything has its own mind?"

"Yep."

"So, why can't I hear the lamppost talking to the drain, or the ground talking to the sky?"

"You haven't been paying attention," said the chocolate wrapper. *"Listen."*

Jennifer listened. She was struck in the face by a hundred voices. Several of them were speaking directly to her.

"Hang on," she said.

She stopped listening. The voices disappeared.

"See what I mean?" said the chocolate wrapper. "It's OK. You just need to learn to control it. Takes a bit of practise."

"OK," said Jennifer. "Thanks."

#

       Jennifer's voice popped into Lester's head like a minor explosion. "Did *you* know about this?"
       "Sorry?"
       "This "everything's alive" thing."
       "I assumed you'd worked that out already," said Lester.
       "I've never needed to work things out," said Jennifer. "I've always assumed I knew everything."
       "Oh."
       "What I don't understand is, of all the thousands of minds that have passed through these doors, how come you're the only person who knows what's really going on out there?"
       "I don't know."
       "What's wrong with your species, Lester?"
       "I couldn't even begin to guess."
       "More to the point, what's wrong with *you?*"
       "There's nothing wrong with me," said Lester.
       "Sorry," said Jennifer. "I'm just trying to understand. You're aware there's a multitude of living beings outside your window, and inside this very room?"
       "Yeah."
       "So, why do you keep yourself locked away from anyone and everyone?"
       "Maybe that's a conversation for another time."
       "Why?"
       "Because I've got no idea how to answer your question."
       "Fine," said Jennifer. "Another time. I've got lots to get on with, anyway."

#

Taking up the chocolate wrapper's advice, Jennifer quickly learned to exercise control over the barrage of information hurtling at her from all directions. She scrutinised the world, one object at a time, engaging in a string of stimulating conversations. If anyone insulted her, she'd block them out completely. If anyone questioned her, she'd engage them in debate. If the conversation became boring, or the debate turned into an argument, she'd politely retreat.
       One thing was for sure – Jennifer would never be alone again.
       She hardly noticed when, on the horizon, an empty office block was toppled by a wrecking ball.

64

There was a man on Jennifer's 55th floor who decided to paint the wall behind his TV. He bought a tin of white paint and a couple of brushes and stuck them on the floor beside the couch.

They were still sitting there the following day.

The man emerged from his bedroom and sat down on the couch. "I really should paint that wall," he said.

He watched TV until nightfall.

The following day, he glanced at the tin of paint, then at the TV. Before he knew it, night had fallen again.

"You watch too much television," he told himself.

He unplugged the TV and dragged it into the wardrobe.

He spent the whole of the following day staring at the blank wall.

The next day, the man went out to buy some bread and milk. He returned to his apartment, made a cup of tea and two slices of toast. He'd used up the last of the margarine, so returned to the shop. He returned home, made another slice of toast and stared at the blank wall until nightfall.

The next day, the man had two cups of tea and one slice of toast. He saved the crusts for later in the day. He looked at the tin of paint and said, "I really should paint that wall."

Night fell.

The following day, he sat on the couch, peered at the tin of paint and said, "I really should paint that wall."

He ate three slices of toast and had four cups of tea. He ran out of teabags so went off to the shop.

He bumped into an old friend.

"Good to see you," she said. "Maybe we could meet up later?"

"I'd love to," he said, "but I'm in the middle of painting my living room."

"Another time, maybe."

He returned to his apartment and made a cup of tea.

By the middle of the next day, he'd grown tired of watching the wall. He opened up the window and scowled at the sky. "At least you don't need repainting," he muttered.

He fell asleep prostrate over the windowsill, his head hanging out into the open air.

He woke up with rain on his face.

He looked up at the sky. "Thanks," he said bitterly.

He shoved his couch round 180 degrees so that it faced the kitchen area. He sat watching the kitchen wall. There were cobwebs in the corners. He stared at the cobwebs.

Night fell.

He woke up on the couch. He shifted position and fell asleep until the afternoon.

He got up to make a cup of tea and a slice of toast, then went to bed.

Night fell.

The following morning, he took a knife from his kitchen drawer and used it to prise open the tin lid.

He fluttered his eyelids as the fumes entered his nostrils.

He turned on the radio, and hummed along to the music as he guided the brush.

By the end of the afternoon, he'd finished the wall. He turned the couch back round. He made a cup of tea, then sat back admiring his work.

Tomorrow he'd make a start at those cobwebs.

65

There was a man who wanted to disappear. His name was Ned Parker.

In his early teens, Ned daydreamed about developing the ability to disintegrate. He'd depart from his body and float away like a swarm of dandelion seeds. He'd monitor the city from close up, while remaining completely detached from it. The obsession progressed throughout his adolescence. By his late twenties, this was no longer a daydream – it was a clear cut ambition.

Ned began visiting Central Library on a regular basis, researching the history of invisibility and its practitioners.

He began with a biography of The Overwhelmer – the magician who'd disappeared without trace at the pinnacle of his career. There was much speculation about the possibility of The Overwhelmer continuing to walk the streets of the Dirty City, fuelled by a number of unsubstantiated sightings.

He discovered a book called *The Undetected: A Study of The Dirty City's Invisible Population* – written, appropriately, by an anonymous author. According to the study, thousands of the city's inhabitants were wandering the streets completely unnoticed by the rest of society – not simply ignored, but literally invisible. It was unclear whether these unseen citizens had become invisible deliberately or not, but the study claimed that by employing the right techniques, anyone could do the same.

Ned read the book from cover to cover a hundred times, returning to the library every few weeks to renew it.

After a year or so, the librarian greeted him at the counter with a knowing smile.

"Here to renew that book again?" he said cheerfully.

"How did you know?" said Ned.

"I can't help noticing you've become a little obsessed with it. Fascinating reading, I'd imagine."

"Have you read it?" said Ned.

"I don't read books," said the librarian. "I catalogue them."

"I see."

The librarian lowered his voice. "I've got some information which may be of interest," he said.

"What information?" said Ned.

"I know what you're trying to do."

"How do you know?"

"I'm perceptive."

"Oh."

"I finish at 6pm if you'd like to come over to my apartment. We can speak in private."

"Sure," said Ned.

\#

At 6pm, Ned followed the librarian silently back to Jennifer. They ascended to the 100th floor.

"Who are you, exactly?" said Ned.

"I'm the oldest man in the world," said the librarian. "Back in a sec."

The oldest man in the world disappeared into the kitchen, returning with a pot of tea with matching cups and saucers.

"Tell me," he said. "What makes you want to disappear?"

"Hmmm," said Ned, blowing softly on his tea. "Tough question. I've just never been interested in participating in communal activity, I suppose. I don't have any friends. Don't use the internet. Don't vote. Don't follow fashion. I'll never be a member of any clubs or societies. I just want to be Ned Parker. As for *why*, I've got no idea. I guess "following the crowd" isn't for everyone."

"So, you actually want to vanish?"

"I don't know why I want to vanish either."

"But you'd like to do it? Given the opportunity?"

"Are you saying you can offer me that?"

The old man smiled like a crackling fire. "I'll tell you a story," he said.

66

It had often been said that Central Library was a haven for people with nowhere better to go. The oldest man in the world was happy to allow homeless people to sleep in his uncomfortable armchairs. He welcomed former businessmen in their crumpled suits, discreetly sipping from hip flasks behind carefully-positioned newspapers.

If the old man had allowed himself to become genuinely interested in his patrons, his attention would most likely have been drawn towards the down-and-outs rather than the conventional bookworms.

One deadbeat in particular proved completely unignorable. The man in question was the first to arrive when the library opened, and was one of the last to leave. Each day, he occupied the same seat in the same corner, reading the same book. The book had a blank cover.

The oldest man in the world expended an incalculable supply of energy resisting the temptation to approach the man and ask him what he was reading. How could any book be so interesting that it demanded to be read that many times?

Eventually, the old man's curiosity got the better of him. He decided to examine the index numbers on the shelf beside the deadbeat's head.

For some reason, it came as no surprise that the pages of the book were completely blank.

The deadbeat quickly snapped the pages shut as soon as he realised the librarian was watching.

"I'm sorry," said the old man, "I was just..."

"It's fine," said the deadbeat.

"Do you mind if I ask...?"

"Why I'm reading a book with blank pages?"

The old man nodded.

"It's called *using your imagination*."

The old man offered a half-smile. "No problem, Mr Tresor."

The deadbeat shot to his feet, dropping his book on the floor. "How do you know?" he whispered furiously.

"I may not look like a Susan Killers fan," said the oldest man in the world, "but I spent enough time listening to you and your band rehearse to recognise a voice like yours. I was rather disappointed to hear you'd split."

"Don't say my name again," said Defo Tresor. "Please."

"Of course not," said the oldest man in the world.

"This conversation never happened."

"Yes it did."

"I think you know what I'm saying."

"Your secret's safe with me," said the old man, "on the condition that you visit for a cup of tea."

"Visit?"

"I live in Jennifer. I assume you still do?"

Defo's face didn't move.

"I'm on the 100th floor," said the old man. Apartment 1459."

With that, he returned to his indexes as though nothing had happened. Defo returned to his empty book.

A couple of evenings later, the old man opened his door to take out the recycling.

Defo Tresor was standing directly outside.

"I'm not a big fan of tea," he said. "I'll take a water."

The old man welcomed him in. "You're a fan of water?" he said.

"Call me pretentious," said Defo, "but even the tap water in the Dirty City has an essence that should never be polluted with caffeine, sugar or alcohol."

"I wouldn't call you pretentious," said the old man. "I'd call you a purist."

Defo took his cup of water, and sipped thoughtfully. "Let me ask you a question, Mr Librarian," he said. "Is there a way an artist can remove himself completely from the work he's created?"

"How do you mean?"

"Take literature, for example. Let's say I wrote a book anonymously. No one, not even close friends or family know that I've written it. Have I removed myself from the work?"

"Not exactly," said the old man. "You're still the author."

"But I'm not the author," said Defo. "I didn't invent storytelling. I didn't invent language. I didn't invent paper. We're *all* the authors. We're all part of the same city, the same world. We share the same history. What's so special about *me?*"

"I suppose the only way to remove yourself completely from your work is to die," said the old man. "Not that I recommend you do so."

"That'd make things a thousand times worse," said Defo. "Can you imagine the obituaries? "We may have lost a genius, but we still have his music" – blah, blah, blah."

"So, you want to cheat death?" said the old man brightly. "You've come to the right place."

"I don't want to die," said Defo, "but I don't want to cheat death either."

"So, what do you want?"

"I want to disappear."

The old man jumped to his feet and began pacing around the room. "Disappear," he murmured. "Disappear." He paced faster. "Dis-app-ear." He quickened his pace. It wasn't long before he was charging around the carpet yelling, *"Disappear! Disappear! Disappear!"*

"What are you doing?" said Defo.

The old man stopped. "Sorry. I appear to be a little over-excited."

"Why?"

The old man sat down again. "Listen," he said. "I don't usually do this sort of thing, but I'd like to tell you a story..."

67

Three centuries ago, there was a movement known as The Transferers. The group was made up of scientists, artists, philosophers and a token bricklayer. Their intention was to devise a way in which each of them could completely vanish. The aim was to continue living in another form – as a liquid or a gas, or a piece of rock – anything that wasn't officially classed as "living". Modern science was in its infancy, and belief in magic was dwindling. The use of scientific methods were one of The Transferers' founding principles. The study of psychology was beginning to become popular among academics. In particular, it had recently been proposed that any feat could be achieved purely through thought.

One member of The Transferers successfully developed the ability to levitate. She flew away before anyone had the opportunity to ask her how she did it.

Another member of the group devised a way of heating himself up to a hundred degrees without breaking a sweat. They used him as a barbecue.

One of The Transferers' founding members dismissed his colleagues' efforts as "party tricks," emphasising the fact that the group was formed with the intention of allowing its members to disappear – or at the very least, alter their physical form. From that point on, the group knuckled down into the serious business of escaping from the world.

As the study of the brain intensified, the concept of "group consciousness" emerged. The Transferers were gripped by the idea that by focussing on their goal, the combined impact of each of their brains would allow them to achieve their objectives.

One of the group – a young musician – volunteered to be a guinea pig. The musician positioned herself at the bottom of a well.

"Are you sure you want to do this?" her colleagues called down. "You're unlikely to find a way back if we're successful."

"Just do me a favour," she said. "Sing the songs I've written – popularise them if you feel they're good enough – but don't tell a single soul that I was the composer."

"No problem," her colleagues called back (although it had to be said, the musician's songs were destined to be forgotten).

She closed her eyes.

Above, her colleagues began to chant – *shed your skin, become the water, shed your bones become the water...*

It was only a matter of minutes before the musician had completely dissolved. The water remained clear.

"What shall we do with it?" said one of the group. "It seems cruel to leave her down a well."

The group agreed. The musician was transferred to a barrel and poured slowly into a river.

In the days that followed, with the assistance of the group, each member disappeared into their chosen form – gold, glass, lava, hydrogen.

Eventually, just one of The Transferers remained. The question of how this member should proceed without the assistance of the group had never been answered.

The man climbed to the top of a mountain where he could have a little privacy. He raised his arms to the sky.

"Shed your skin," he said, *"become the air, shed your bones, become the air."*

Three days later, he was still there.

68

"What happened to him?" said Defo.

The librarian slowly raised his hand. "I may not have mentioned," he said, "but I'm the oldest man in the world."

There were several minutes of contemplative silence.

"How've you managed to live so long?" said Defo eventually.

"Basically, it involves avoiding interestingness," said the old man. "You may not realise this, Defo, but sitting in a room with you is a very dangerous thing."

"If you're avoiding interestingness," said Defo, "how come you became a member of The Transferers?"

"It was a means to an end," said the old man. "Ultimately I wanted to avoid people altogether. Sadly, not only had I failed to evaporate, I'd become terminally interesting."

Defo looked the old man up and down. "Doesn't seem to have been that terminal," he said.

"I suppose so. Anyway, do you fancy another water?"

"Sure."

The old man disappeared into the kitchen, returning with a pair of cups on a china tray.

"So, what do you think?" he said.

"About...?"

"About disappearing. I'm happy to help. I've done it before."

Another uncomfortable pause.

"I've got a bathtub," said the old man helpfully. "Only if you want to."

"A bathtub?"

"You'll need time to think about it, of course."

"I've thought about it," said Defo. "I've done nothing but think about it since the first time I plucked a guitar string."

"Think about it some more. Give it twenty four hours at least."

#

The following day, when the librarian arrived for work, the first person he saw was Defo sitting in the corner, reading his book.

"What are you doing here?" said the old man.

"I'm thinking," said Defo.

The old man glanced down at the page. It said: *Do it, do it, do it, do it, do it, do it...*

#

That evening, the old man opened his door to take out his glass bottles. Defo was standing staring at his door.

"I want to do it," he said.

\#

"So, you did it?" said Ned Parker. "You dissolved the lead singer of the Susan Killers?"

"Were you a fan?"

"No, but there are quite a few people who'd be pretty upset."

The old man shrugged. "It's what he wanted. I helped him achieve his life's ambition."

"What did you do with the water?"

"Pulled out the plug," said the old man. "It was Defo's request."

"Did he have any last words?"

"Yes. I remember them very clearly. He said, "Forget me, Mr Librarian.""

"And you haven't."

"I've wilfully forgotten most of the interesting moments of my life, but I couldn't forget that."

"I understand," said Ned.

"So, what do you think?" said the old man. "I can do the same for you if that's what you really want."

Ned smiled for the first time since his arrival. "It is," he said.

69

And so, Ned Parker dissolved himself and entered the city's waterways.
He was flushed into The Sludge.
He evaporated and was rained into the street.
Eventually, he ended up racing through Jennifer's plumbing system.
He was poured into a glass on the 47th floor.
Lester drank him.
He called down to Ned a moment later.
"Hello?" said Lester. "Am I right in thinking I've just swallowed a human being?"
"Er ... yeah," said Ned. "Very perceptive of you."
"How's it going?"
"It's going very well, I suppose," said Ned. "I haven't been doing much thinking or feeling, to be honest. I've just been doing stuff. Floating, running, sitting in puddles – things like that."
"What's that like?"
"Not quite what I suspected," said Ned. "I don't mean to complain, but all I've ever wanted to do is keep my head down and stay out of trouble. Didn't exactly work out as planned."
"So I can see."
"Anyway, I'll leave you to it," said Ned. "I'll be out of your system in a couple of days."

#

A couple of days passed, and Ned departed, leaving a small trace of himself behind. Everywhere he travelled, tiny smudges of Ned Parker were deposited until bits of him covered everything and everyone. Wherever you were in the city, you were never two feet away from Ned Parker. He saw everything, heard everything, felt everything. He was everything.
The next time he entered Lester's body through Jennifer's plumbing system, he was much more upbeat.
"My friend," he said, "if you ever want to gain an appreciation of how everything's connected, turn yourself into a bathful of water and flush yourself down the drain. There's a guy on the 100th floor who can sort you out."
"I'll leave it for now," said Lester, "but thanks for the tip."
Ned responded wordlessly with a smile that stretched across a hundred pipes.

70

The oldest woman in the world was seventeen weeks younger than her male counterpart. Somehow the two of them had never met, despite having lived in relatively close proximity for the majority of their four-digit lifetimes.

One afternoon, the oldest woman in the world was sitting on a park bench imagining patterns on the grassless lawn when Eliza sat down beside her. She'd only stopped to tie her laces, but the bench turned out to be more comfortable than it looked.

"Don't mind me," she said. "I might breathe heavily for a while."

The oldest woman in the world offered a cheeky grin. "Running away from something, are we?"

"Just jogging, thanks," said Eliza.

"How fast can you run, *Slumber Fairy?*"

Eliza jumped to her feet and considered breaking into a sprint.

She stopped, turning to examine the conspiratorial expression on the old woman's face. "How do you know?" she said.

"Believe it or not," said the old woman, "I've been alive several centuries longer than the city itself. Experience has made me more perceptive than most."

Eliza glanced over her shoulder.

"It's OK," said the old woman. "No one's listening."

"You're not gonna grass me up?"

"Eliza, you know as well as I do, there's no one to "grass you up" to."

Eliza took a step closer, and lowered her tone. "You *are* perceptive, aren't you?" she said.

"It's what comes with being the oldest woman in the world."

"How do you know you're the oldest woman in the world?"

"I'll change my opinion when I meet someone older than me."

"Fair enough. Good to meet you."

With that, Eliza skipped on the spot, ready to set off running again. "See you later."

"Hang on," said the old woman. "You don't get away that easily."

"Eh?"

"You can't admit to being the Slumber Fairy and then disappear without sharing a couple of stories."

"I understand," said Eliza, sitting down slowly. "How about you go first."

"Why?" said the old woman.

"I get the impression you've got *way* more stories than me. Go for it."

The old woman whispered in her ear: "Not here. Come up to my apartment."

"Where do you live?"
"Jennifer. 63rd floor."

#

The living room was sparsely furnished, with dusty, unpainted walls. The place smelt of mouldy potatoes.

The old woman made a cup of tea, then presented Eliza with an enormous biscuit barrel with rust at the edges.

"Nice," said Eliza. "Clearly we've got a *lot* of stories to get through."

"Where do you want me to start?" said the old woman. "Not the beginning, I hope."

"OK," said Eliza. "Let's start at the end."

"I couldn't possibly tell you how my story's going to finish," said the old woman. "But I dare say my future's secured."

"What makes you say that?"

The old woman smiled through a mouthful of crumbs. "I had no intention of telling anyone this, but between the two of us, I'm not just the oldest woman in this city – I'm also one of the richest."

"No surprise there, I suppose," said Eliza. "I'm guessing you've got a decent savings account?"

"Nope. Don't believe in banks."

"So, how did you make your money?"

The old woman winked theatrically. "Good honest gambling, my dear. It was only recently that I cottoned onto this knack that I have of predicting future events against all probability. That's when I won 6 million dollars on the Lottery. I bet every single cent on a horse that was a 100-1 outsider."

"Something tells me you won, right?"

The old woman nodded.

"So what did you spend it on?"

"*Invested* is probably a better word. I developed an interest in the stock market."

"Wow," said Eliza. "I can see where this is going."

"I officially retired when I reached the twelve billion mark. It seemed as good a figure as any."

"Hang on," said Eliza. "How come you're still living in Jennifer?"

The old woman shrugged. "It's a small apartment, but it suits my needs. Couldn't be doing with anything bigger. The rent's pretty reasonable."

"You're *renting?*"

"Seems easier."

"But you've got twelve billion dollars."

"It might sound like a lot to you," said the old lady. "This is my pension fund. I've got nothing apart from my savings."

"I'd say you're sorted," said Eliza.

"My dear, you're forgetting my ability to carry on living. I'm not giving up yet."

"How long are you planning on being alive?"

"I don't know," said the old woman. "I've set myself an allowance of ten thousand a year. How long will that get me?"

Eliza pulled out her phone and tapped in some numbers. "12,000,000,000 divided by 10,000," she said. "Without taking inflation into account, that'll give you enough for 120,000 years."

"OK," said the old woman. "We'll see what society looks like in 120,000 years time. If such a thing as money still exists, I'd better start gambling again."

"I like your attitude."

"Thank you."

"Wait a minute," said Eliza. "Did you say you haven't got a bank account?"

"Nope."

"So, you're in possession of twelve billion dollars *in cash?*"

"I haven't got it sewn into my mattress if that's what you think," said the old woman.

"Where do you keep it, then?"

"I rent the apartment next door."

"Of course you do."

"I hope you don't think I'm just some crazy old dear. I'm a revolutionary. Imagine if everyone withdrew their money from the banks. No debt, no inflation, no interest. Power to the people."

"Cool."

"I can show you next door if you like."

Eliza remained in her seat.

"What's wrong?" said the old woman.

"I don't know," said Eliza. "For some reason, it's kind of *scary*."

"Come on, my dear. I'd like someone else to see."

Obligingly, Eliza followed the old woman through the door into the neighbouring apartment.

"So," she said quietly. "This is what twelve billion dollars looks like."

71

The day after meeting the oldest woman in the world, Eliza let herself into Lester's apartment and began charging around the carpet.
"Hello," said Lester.
"Hello."
"What are you doing?"
"Pacing."
"Why?"
"Helps me think."
"What are you thinking about?"
Eliza told him the story of the oldest woman in the world.
"I see your dilemma," he said.
"How do you know I had a dilemma?"
"You've found an apartment housing twelve billion dollars."
"So?"
"You're a highly-skilled burglar."
"Lester, I've never stolen a penny in my life."
"Doesn't mean you're not capable of doing so. It's not like the old lady would mind if a portion of it went missing. If you took half of it off her hands, she probably wouldn't even notice for another sixty thousand years."
"Yes, but what about the principle?"
"Is it the principle that's bothering you?"
"No."
"Why did you mention it then?"
"Because it feels like I ought to."
"What's actually bothering you?"
"I *like* her," said Eliza. "I think we could end up being friends. Under normal circumstances, I'd happily steal a couple of billion, but I'd never be able to see her again."
"Why?"
"She'd be able to tell."
"How do you know?"
"Didn't you listen to the story? She's *perceptive*, Lester."
"Oh."
"What do you mean?"
"Just thinking," said Lester. "Looks like you've set yourself a challenge."
"Eh?"
"Stealing a couple of billion – that's the easy part. Turning up on the old lady's doorstep as though nothing's happened – that's a risk you'll have to take."
Eliza stopped pacing and marched right up to him. "Since when have you been the devil on my shoulder, Lester?"
"I'm just saying what you're thinking."
"How do you know what I'm thinking?"

"I don't know. Maybe I'm perceptive."
"Don't *you* start."

72

The following afternoon, Eliza stole two billion dollars in cash from apartment 627. After stuffing the bundled notes into a bag under her bed at home, she returned to Jennifer's 63rd floor.

The oldest woman in the world appeared pleasantly surprised to find Eliza on her doorstep. "Good to see you again," she greeted. Her smile was impossible to read. Maybe it was the false teeth.

"So, I'd better make myself comfortable," said Eliza. "How many stories have you got?"

"How much time do you have?"

"Not as much as you, I'd imagine."

They laughed.

"Anyway," said the old woman, "It's your turn now. I want to hear the kind of dreams the Slumber Fairy had access to."

"No problem," said Eliza. "What sort of dream do you want to hear about?"

"I don't know. You pick. Something that would appeal to me."

"Here we go..."

#

There was a woman on Jennifer's 88th floor.

In a dream, she descended to the ground in the middle of the night, stepping out onto the expanse of flat dull concrete that formed Jennifer's perimeter.

She pulled a brick from her pocket and laid it on the ground.

She woke up.

The following night, she stepped outside, pulled a brick from her pocket and placed it next to the first brick.

She woke up.

The process continued. After a few days, she'd formed a small square. The next night she began building a second layer.

She continued laying down a single brick each night. Sometimes she'd break the trend and pull a brick from each pocket.

As weeks and months passed, the building grew higher. She began using a stepladder. As the nights wore on, she extended her ladder to match the height of the building.

A couple of years later, the top of the tower drew parallel with her apartment on the 88th floor. For a few nights, she just sat at her window gazing out at her creation. Then the work resumed.

Two more years went by. The woman's tower was almost twice the size of Jennifer.

One night, instead of climbing the ladder and laying down another brick, she stood at the bottom, looking up.

She folded up the ladder.

The following night, the woman stepped out into the dark, and looked up again. It had been some time since she'd allowed herself the opportunity to stand back and admire her handiwork. She stood in the same spot until morning.

The following night, the woman walked right past the tower. She strode through the empty streets until she arrived at an abandoned construction site.

She helped herself to the biggest truck she could find, and sped back to Jennifer.

The tower toppled into the dark, whistling through the breeze as it fell.

She woke up.

The following night, she stepped out into the concrete wasteland.

She pulled a brick from her pocket and placed in on the ground.

#

"Interesting," said the oldest woman in the world. "What does it mean?"

"I don't know," said Eliza. "Sometimes the meaningless ones have the biggest impact."

"Doesn't it mean…?"

"No. It doesn't mean anything."

"Fine. Next please."

73

There was a kitten who had a dream about rescuing a fire fighter from a tree.

The kitten had never seen a tree in real life. In her imagination, it was roughly the size of Jennifer. The fire fighter was around halfway up, stuck at the end of a flimsy branch, which was likely to snap under his weight at any moment.

"Need any help up there?" called the kitten.

"I'm sorry," called the fire fighter.

"Don't apologise," called the kitten as she clawed her way up.

"It's pretty humiliating, to be honest," he said.

"No need to be embarrassed," said the kitten. "There's only you and me here."

"Suppose so."

"How did you get this high in the first place?"

"Just trying to impress my mates. Dropped my phone halfway through a selfie."

"It's fine."

The kitten leapt casually onto the branch. The fire fighter was sobbing softly.

"Come on," she said. "We've all got our weak spots. You're good at putting out fires – I'm good at climbing trees. If there's a lesson to be learned here…"

"Don't patronise me," said the fire fighter, brushing off his tears with a pair of clenched fists. "You're a *kitten*."

"Do you want to be rescued or not?"

"No," he replied firmly. "I'll stay up here forever if I have to."

"You can hang onto my back. I'm surprisingly powerful for a creature my size."

"Leave me alone."

"Your choice I suppose," said the kitten.

In a series of casually acrobatic leaps, she swung her way back to ground.

She returned a couple of minutes later. The fire fighter's hands were over his eyes.

"I brought your phone," she said.

The fire fighter pulled his hands from his face. "Thank you," he said.

"You're sure I can't assist you?"

"Look, I appreciate all this, but…"

"No shame in asking for help."

"Shut up."

"Consider my offer at least."

"No!" yelled the fire fighter. He threw back his arm, hurling his phone at the ground. There was a distant shatter. "No!" he shouted. *"No, no, no, no, no, no, no, no, NO!"*

The kitten jumped back to ground in a single step.

"Hmmm," said the old woman.

"Honestly," said Eliza, "don't try and analyse it."

"I can't help thinking the fire fighter is a projection of the kitten's own inner struggle. Fierce independence verses a reliance on her owner's supply of canned meat."

"Seriously?" said Eliza.

"You don't think so?"

"I can see your train of thought. Dreams are a window into our deepest fears and desires, right? I agree, as it happens. But sometimes a dream's just a dream."

"Let's dig deeper then," said the old woman. "Give me something that makes sense."

"You asked for it," said Eliza.

74

There was a Peeping Tom on Jennifer's 79th floor. He called himself The Observer.

The Observer had a hidden camera in his bathroom, overlooking his shower. He didn't place it there himself. The camera was tiny enough to be slotted into a hairline crack between the wall and the ceiling. The average occupant could be forgiven for failing to notice. Whoever his stalker was, they clearly knew what they were up to.

The Observer was perfectly comfortable with this arrangement. He was rather flattered that someone had gone to the trouble of spying on him. He often wondered if the people he spied on would feel the same about him if he were ever to reveal himself.

He often spoke to the camera at length, detailing his numerous breaches of privacy and hypothesising over who the owner of the camera may have been.

One night, The Observer dreamt that he was moving to another one of Jennifer's apartments.

He packed up his belongings, boxed up his huge collection of illicit photographs, and carted them off to his new place, a couple of floors up.

He offered a parting farewell to the camera. "I'm tempted to take you with me," he said. "But if your owners are paying attention – and why wouldn't they be? – they'll know where to find me."

He winked, and departed.

A short while later, he took a shower in his new apartment. As he did so, he noticed a hairline crack between the ceiling and the wall. He fell on his back.

Too shocked to feel pain, he jumped up, towelled himself dry and ran to grab a magnifying glass from his suitcase.

He returned to the bathroom and stood on the toilet seat.

As he'd suspected, an identical camera had been installed in his new bathroom.

He'd only been given the keys to the apartment that afternoon. Logically, there was no way his fellow Peeping Tom could've installed the hidden camera so quickly after him moving in. *Unless...*

He fell on his back again.

He lay in thoughtful silence.

At this point, the sleeping Observer rolled over in his bed, mumbling something to himself about the ridiculousness of his own subconscious before falling asleep again.

The dream resumed where it had left off.

The Observer jumped to his feet. He grabbed a spanner from his suitcase, left the apartment and ran up the stairs. He hammered on the door of the nearest apartment to the stairwell.

An elderly man peeped through the letterbox. "Can I help you?" he said.

The Observer waved the spanner. "Emergency plumber," he said. "There's been a leak upstairs."

"Oh dear," said the old man, opening the door.

"I need to inspect your shower," he said, still wielding the spanner.

"Just through there," he said.

The Observer ran into the bathroom and stood on the toilet seat. He inspected the hairline crack between the ceiling and the wall. A micro-lens peered at his face.

He repeated his "emergency plumber" routine with the next five apartments. The story was the same in each: tiny camera after tiny camera.

The Observer woke up. Without a moment's hesitation, he jumped out of bed, pulled a pair of tweezers from his drawer and took them into the bathroom. He rammed the tweezers into the crack in the ceiling, opening it wide enough to yank out the offending device, dropping it into the toilet. Plaster dust rained over his hair.

The camera was small enough to disappear in a single flush.

Thinking about his hasty decision later in the day, The Observer wondered why he'd been so outraged. Was it the thought that there was an even more prolific spy than himself operating inside Jennifer? It was enough to make any voyeur jealous.

More likely it was a sense of betrayal. He'd lost the sense of intimacy that accompanied the notion that his mystery viewer had chosen him over everyone else. Now it appeared that the whole building was being indiscriminately observed.

But, of course, it was all just a dream. The Observer had destroyed the camera in reaction to an imaginary event.

He spent the remainder of the day lying on his bathroom floor looking up at the hole in the ceiling.

#

"As it happens," said the old woman, "The Observer spied on me for a while. Poor little devil didn't realise I was onto him."

"So, you've spied on him too?" said Eliza. "Surely it wasn't you who...?"

"Definitely not my scene," said the old woman with a firm shake of the head.

"How did you feel about being watched against your will?"

"It's not so bad if you're aware that it's happening. I can't bring myself to feel any animosity towards him. To his credit, he's fully aware that my other apartment is loaded with cash. The thought of discreetly helping himself to a couple of wads has never even occurred to him. There aren't many people like that. The majority of the population wouldn't steal it, but I reckon most would at least consider it for a split second. It's only natural. Wouldn't you agree?"

Eliza blinked hard. "Yeah," she said.

75

"She knows," said Eliza.

"How can you tell?" said Lester.

"Her expression."

"So, what's she going to do?"

"Nothing. I'm guessing I'm officially pardoned. It's a shame I can't bring myself to go back there again. At least I've got you, Lester."

A wave of comfortable silence rushed over them.

"Yeah," said Lester.

A further wave descended.

"What are you gonna do with the money?" he said.

"I don't know. I'm tempted to put it back, but then it'll just be sitting there. Maybe I should nick the whole lot and donate it to charity. What do you think?"

"Dunno."

"Oh, come off it, Lester. Surely you must have an opinion in there somewhere. Tell me something. *Anything.* What do you *think?*"

"I've always had problems with opinions," said Lester. "I don't really feel qualified to make a judgement."

"Come on – we've spoken about this. You can understand the difference between right and wrong, yeah?"

"Yeah. Murdering people's wrong – there's an opinion for you. Jeremy Mercer killed all the plants – that's wrong too. It's the grey areas I can't handle. I try to avoid dilemmas. They annoy me."

"They're part of *life*, Lester."

"Not *my* life."

"Fine. You carry on ignoring everything."

"I'm not ignoring anything," said Lester.

"You're ignoring my question," said Eliza. "What shall I do with the money? For once in your life, Lester, try and have a gut reaction."

"My gut reaction?" said Lester. "I think you should ignore your gut reaction, whatever it happens to be. I think you should think about it, long and hard."

Silence resumed, less comfortably than before.

"You're right," said Eliza. "Damn it."

76

One day, the oldest woman in the world decided to join the library. She tried to retain as few possessions as possible, so borrowing books rather than buying them seemed like the way to go.

"Hello madam," said the oldest man in the world.

"Hello sir," said the oldest woman in the world. "I woke up this morning and realised I haven't read a book for *centuries*."

"Me neither."

"So, I thought I'd investigate what the kids are writing nowadays."

"No problem. There's a form to fill in, I'm afraid."

She tutted playfully. "Bureaucracy, eh? If I could total up the number of hours I've spent completing application forms…"

"Life's too short," he agreed.

The old woman quickly jotted down her details.

As she did so, the old man glanced at the form and steadied himself on his stool.

Speechlessly, he gestured towards her date of birth.

The old woman leant forward and whispered in his ear. "It's not a mistake. I'm over a thousand years old."

The old man struggled to breathe for a moment.

"It's OK," she said. "Steady."

She took him by the hand, which seemed to relax him a little.

"Do you realise," he said, "we were born one hundred and nineteen days apart?"

She whistled casually. "One hundred and nineteen, eh?"

"You're not shocked?"

"Nah. I've seen too much in my life to be surprised by anything."

"How funny," he said. "I've seen too little. *Everything* surprises me."

"I can see we've got a lot to catch up on," she said. "Would you like to go out for dinner tonight?"

The old man replied with the faintest trace of enthusiasm. "Why ever not?"

#

They had a gapless conversation all evening. The old woman did most of the talking.

"I've been married ninety-eight times," she said. "Not a single divorce."

"Not bad going," he said. "So, let me get this right – you've been widowed *ninety-eight times?* Either that or you're a prolific bigamist."

"You get used to being widowed after the first few deaths," she said. "You start appreciating the inevitability. We'll all cease to exist one day – even you and I."

"Not if I can help it."

"The point is, all relationships are short-term. Ever been married?"

"No. Too interesting."

"Too what?"

"It's how I've survived this long. I've avoided interestingness."

"You didn't necessarily have to do that. I'm kind of interesting, and I'm still around."

"So, how do you keep going?"

The oldest woman in the world flashed one of her trademark winks. "*Stubbornness*, my dear," she said.

They laughed.

At the end of the evening, he escorted her to her door.

"I had a great time tonight," he said. "When can we do this again?"

"Let's not be too hasty," she said. "I'm not looking for anything permanent."

His eyes slumped half-shut. "I thought you said all relationships are short-term."

"Ordinarily they are," she said.

"Oh," he said. "Ah. I see what you mean."

"Perhaps we should hook up in a couple of decades. Maybe make it a regular thing every twenty years."

"I'll give you a knock," he said.

She leant forward and kissed him gently on the cheek. "It's a date."

77

"So, come on," said Jennifer. "Tell me why you're so happy on your own."

"Why do you always begin conversations in the middle?" said Lester.

"Sorry," said Jennifer. "Hello."

"Hello Jennifer."

"Well? Surely you've had time to think about the question."

"As it happens, yes I have. Would you like me to show you something?"

"Yes please," said Jennifer.

Lester closed his eyes. Jennifer was about to prompt him with another question, when an invisible force grabbed her, commanding the attention of every ounce of her energy.

As Lester's mind opened up, story after story assaulted her, forcing themselves into her consciousness like unordered slugs of whiskey.

When the waves of fiction subsided, the centre of Lester's mind was revealed, appearing as a star-like ball of flame.

It spoke to her: "You see now?"

All Jennifer could manage to say was, "Oh."

She stared at the ball of flame a while longer before adding, "What are you?"

"I'm the truth," said the ball.

"Oh yes. Of course. Didn't recognise you."

"Not many people do."

Slowly, the light was eclipsed as Lester bricked up the walls of his mind once again.

"You could've warned me," said Jennifer once she'd regained the power of speech. "You've got that thing living inside you?"

"Everyone does, don't they?" said Lester.

Jennifer considered this observation for an hour or so. Then she said, "Thank you, Lester. You've answered my question."

"You've woken me up again," said Lester.

"Sorry," said Jennifer. "I won't disturb you any further."

"Thanks."

"Just one thing," said Jennifer. "*Never* show me the core of your being again. I think I've been scarred for life."

"You asked for it."

"I know I did."

"Goodnight Jennifer."

"Goodnight."

78

There was an office in a basement, a couple of floors below Jennifer's ground, in which a man was paid to sit in an old armchair watching action films. His official job title was Lost Property Officer, but seen as very few possessions were reported as missing, and even fewer were handed in, TV was his main occupation.

One day, the Lost Property Officer was distracted by a phone call.

On the screen, a cop was being thrown from the roof of a building by a pair of heavily-built criminals with their chests out.

The cop landed on the roof of a car, almost chopping the vehicle in two. He groaned and pulled himself to his feet. He picked up his gun, dusted himself off and headed back inside the building.

In the real world, the phone continued to ring. Reluctantly, the Lost Property Officer answered: "Can I help you?"

"Sorry to bother you," said a woman's voice. "I seem to have lost my wallet."

"Have you looked in your apartment?" said the Lost Property Officer.

"I can't find it," said the woman. "That's why I'm calling you."

"You understand the lost property department is only responsible for items that are lost in communal areas?"

"I do understand that," said the woman. "That's why I'm calling."

The Lost Property Officer paused the TV as he took down the woman's details.

He hung up and pressed play.

The cop punched the button to call the elevator, busting it off the wall. He made a run for the stairs. He sprinted his way to the stop in the space of thirty seconds.

He apprehended the two topless bodybuilders, bashed their heads together and threw them off the building.

Another call came through.

"Yeah?" said the Lost Property Officer.

"Hi," said a man. "I'm wondering if you can help. I've lost my credit cards."

"No credit cards here," said the Lost Property Officer.

"Maybe you could take down my details," said the man.

"OK," said the officer wearily, pausing the TV.

Immediately after hanging up the phone, another call came through. He snatched up the handset.

"This isn't funny," he said. "I'm trying to *work* here."

"Sorry?" said a voice.

"If this is a *joke*..."

"This is the Lost Property Office, right?"

"Don't tell me. You've lost your wallet."

"Ah, you've found it!" said the voice.

"No," said the Lost Property Officer. "Lucky guess. I'll take down your details."

The voice dictated its name and phone number. The officer didn't bother writing them down.

#

The pattern continued over the next few days. A multitude of wallets, watches, jewellery and cash were reported missing, none of which had been handed in.

Eventually, the Lost Property Officer decided to divert all calls to voicemail. The messages mounted up. He deleted them.

The next day, there was a knock at the door.

"Yeah?" called the Lost Property Officer.

A woman walked in. "Hi," she said.

"Sorry," said the Lost Property Officer, not looking up from the TV. "We don't take face to face queries."

"I left a message," said the woman. "I was wondering if you picked it up?"

"Yours and everyone else's," said the Lost Property Officer. "Sorry, but nothing's been handed in. Hundreds of items have vanished. Don't ask me where they're all going."

"Maybe there's a thief in the building," said the woman.

"Several thieves, I'd imagine," he said.

His face jerked away from the TV. "Hang on," he said. "That's it, isn't it? We should let the police deal with it! Thank you, madam, you've saved me a lot of time and effort."

He took down the woman's details and sent her on her way.

He picked up the phone and called the police.

He was put on hold.

After 15 minutes or so, a voice said, "How can I help?"

"I'd like to report a series of thefts," said the Lost Property Officer. He began reeling off a list of the names he'd been bothered to make a note of.

"One moment, sir," said the voice. "We can only do these one at a time. Each theft will need to be assigned a unique crime reference number."

"Oh."

"So, the first person you listed – you said they've lost their wallet, is that correct?"

"Yes."

"Can you tell me what was in the wallet at the time?"

"No idea."

"And where do they live?"

"Jennifer."

"Which apartment?"

"684."

"If you'd like to make a note of the reference number – do you have a pen?"
"Yeah."
"It's B12578FFK9. We'll contact the individual in due course."
"You know," said the Lost Property Officer, "you people are nothing like the cops on TV."

79

After a lengthy phone call with the Lost Property Officer, the series of suspected thefts were assigned to a police officer named Spool.

Spool began his investigation by inspecting the security footage from the hidden Automated Interpretive Video Capture cameras in and around Jennifer.

Over many cups of coffee and several sausage rolls, Spool trawled his way through hours of security footage. Firstly, he established that a large number of incidents had taken place directly outside the building. Secondly, he established that each of these attacks had been carried out by one individual. Thirdly, he established that the culprit lived somewhere in Jennifer.

He spent the next few days camped outside the building watching the live AIVC footage through his phone.

With no sign of the thief, Spool called the Lost Property Office.

"Yeah?" came the answer.

"Hi. My name's Spool – I'm a police officer."

"If you don't mind, I'm in the middle of something."

Spool detected the sound of a simulated gun battle in the background. "This'll just take a second," he said. "Can I check how many items have been reported missing in the last few days?"

"Nothing, thankfully," said the Lost Property Officer.

"Right. Thanks."

Spool hung up and dialled another number.

Eliza picked up. "Hello?" she said.

"Hi," said Spool. "Don't panic. This is the police. You may remember me..."

"Of course I remember you, Spool."

Spool was pleased she wasn't around to see him blush. "I..."

"Is this about the drink?"

"It's not about the drink," he said quickly. "I need your help. I mean, it would be useful if you could assist me with my enquiries."

"Sure," said Eliza.

"I think you'll be interested in watching this..."

#

Spool treated Eliza to a coffee and a specially-purchased cheese and onion roll before escorting her into his darkened room. He played her a selection of slow-motion videos. Eliza watched in silence, casually sipping on her drink.

The footage of each of the crimes was played out from three angles. In one, the pickpocket was personified as an eagle. Camera two was a child on a skateboard. Camera three was a bolt of lightning.

"Little devil," she said softly.

"I had to look twice when I watched this," said Spool. "I assumed I'd accidentally switched to high speed. When you were mugged, I couldn't figure out why camera three had chosen a lightning bolt. I'd never seen an AIVC camera do that before. I understand now. This guy is *literally* that fast. No wonder no one noticed their possessions being stolen."

Eliza was still staring at the screen.

"What do you think?" said Spool.

"I think we've discovered the greatest pickpocket of all time."

"I can see you're impressed."

"Sorry. I know I'm not supposed to be."

"I don't blame you," said Spool. "Frankly, I'm bowled over by the genius of the man."

"What makes you think it's a man?"

Spool shrugged.

"Have you got any actual footage? Using a real camera, I mean."

"Er..."

"I'll take that as a no."

"We probably look incompetent, don't we?"

"Are there any actual *cameras* in this city?"

"There's a few," said Spool. "I suspect our friend Eagle Boy knows where they are, and avoids them. He deliberately steals people's possessions in front of the AIVC cameras. Every single one of these crimes is in clear view. He wants us to watch him."

"Why?" said Eliza.

"You know why," said Spool.

"Do I?"

"He's showing off."

"How would I know that?"

"Takes one to know one."

"You think *I'm* a show-off? You're the one who brought me in so you could brag about your fancy cameras and your empty prison."

"Like I say, it takes one to know one."

"We're not talking about you and me – we're talking about Eagle Boy. And I disagree, by the way. He doesn't look like he's showing off. He's doing it for his own amusement."

"You don't think he needs the money, then?"

"My guess is, he's pretty well-off. If he was poor, he could use his expertise to carry out a more substantial crime. I'm sure he could rob a bank without much effort."

"If he's rich, why does he live in Jennifer?"

"The Canvas isn't for everyone."

"Suppose not."

Eliza sat back in her seat and shoved the final crumbs of pastry into her mouth. "Listen," she said. "Why don't you just camp outside until Eagle Boy strikes again?"

"Tried that," said Spool. "The thefts stopped as soon as I arrived."

"So, he's onto you?"

Spool looked at the wall. "I think so."

Eliza span around in her chair a few times. "Just wondering ... these AIVC things. How small are they?"

"Pretty titchy," said Spool. "Makes them easy to hide."

"Is there a handheld version?"

"Why do you ask?"

"Don't ask. Just lend me one."

Spool smiled. "I knew you could help me out. How long do you need it for?"

"A few weeks, I guess."

"Sounds like a lot of work. What kind of payment are you expecting?"

"Nothing. Happy to help."

Spool attempted to study Eliza's expression. "What do you do for a living, Eliza?"

"Don't ask," she said. "Just get me the camera."

"OK."

80

It was late in the evening when the oldest woman in the world received a knock on her door.

"It's a good job I was awake," she said as her face popped into view.

"Sorry," said Eliza.

"What's that?" said the old woman.

"Camera. Pretty funky, eh?"

"Is that an AIVC?"

"How do you know?"

"You'd better come in. Got a story for you."

"Cool," said Eliza, following the old woman into the living room.

"Fancy a biscuit?"

"Later on. I'd like to crack on with the story if that's alright."

The old lady shook her head. "Ah, you youngsters – you act like you're going to die tomorrow."

"Sorry," said Eliza.

The old lady handed her the biscuit tin. "So…" she said.

#

Automated Interpretive Video Capture was created by an IT technician called Samuel Proust in his apartment in Jennifer.

He began by building a computer made of marble. Being an eccentric type, Proust's friends assumed it was an elaborate practical joke, which would presumably become funny at some point.

"Isn't this going to be incredibly time consuming?" one friend asked. "Considering the intricacies of the system, and the difficulty you'll have carving them…"

As if to prove her wrong, Proust finished the job in a matter of days. He invited his friend over to his apartment.

"How does this work?" she said.

Proust addressed the computer: "Is there a God?"

The computer extended a mechanised arm and etched its response on a small chalkboard. "Not in my opinion, but who's to say?"

"Did you programme it to say that?" said his friend.

"No," said Proust. "This is as much a surprise to me as it is to you."

"So, basically, you've created a machine with its own opinions? Its own feelings?"

"I'm not sure about feelings," said Proust. He addressed the computer. "How are you feeling?"

"Alright," etched the computer. "I suppose I should be overwhelmed about having just been born, but I'm more apathetic than anything else. Maybe a little disappointed."

"So, you've got an emotional response, but it's not as strong as a human's would be?"

"Yeah. Suppose."

"What do you reckon?" Proust asked his friend.

His friend was speechless for a couple of minutes.

"You'll be a very rich man," she said, when she'd come to her senses.

"I would if I wanted to sell it," said Proust. "I think I'd better patent the idea and ensure no one ever manufactures it."

"Shame," she said.

She gazed at the sparkling slab.

"So, how does it work?" she said after a while.

"Not sure," said Proust. "There's something special about marble."

"I see what you mean."

"Do you think I can find a material that'd be more emotionally pliable?" he said.

"No idea," she said.

"I'll give it a go."

#

After a few weeks locked away in his apartment, Proust gathered a small group of friends together to reveal his next masterpiece. In the most sophisticated origami construction of all time, Proust created an intelligent, emotional and well-balanced being with an interest in philosophy and professional darts. It was made entirely of paper.

Speculation quickly spread, against Proust's best wishes. Evidently his friends had bigger mouths than he'd hoped. It wasn't long before scientists and company bosses were calling with job offers and eight-figure sums in exchange for his design. They were met with a simple "No thank you."

One day, Proust received a phone call from Jeremy Mercer, who was part way through a short stint as Justice Minister.

"I'm not going to ask you about your computer," said Mercer.

"That's what I call a promising start to a conversation."

"I'm interested in *you*, Mr Proust. The Ministry of Justice needs men like yourself. Men who want to make a difference."

"What makes you think that's my intention?"

"Why else would you refuse to disclose the secret of your emotionally intelligent origami? You've eliminated the possibility of society being destroyed by artificial intelligence. I applaud you for that."

"It's not because I want to make a difference," said Proust. "It's because I want the world to remain the same."

"OK, let's forget all that for now. Let's talk about crime fighting."

"Why should I care about crime fighting?"

"Surely you agree that thugs and killers should be brought to justice?"

"Not really," said Proust. "There's nothing quite as exciting as an unsolved murder case. Makes great television."

Mercer whistled down the line. "My, my," he said. "It's not often I meet someone as emotionally bankrupt as I am."

"Pleased to meet you," said Proust.

"Let me be honest," said Mercer. "I need to bump our arrest rates up, and frankly, I'm out of ideas. I suspect I'm wasting my time with this question, but have you ever thought of incorporating your computer into another kind of device? Something we could use as part of criminal investigations? "

"Interesting," said Proust. "Give me a day or two."

"Wow."

"Sorry?"

Mercer coughed. "Nothing," he said. "I just wasn't expecting a positive response."

"You're a little different to the others," said Proust. "They all offered me money. What you've offered me, Mr Mercer, is a *challenge*."

#

"… and so, a couple of days later, Automated Interpretive Video Capture was born."

"So, these things have got *paper* in them?" said Eliza.

"You'd better be careful with that thing."

"I will be."

"What are you doing with it anyway?"

"I was wondering if you could help me."

"My, I like the sound of this already!"

"You don't even know what it is yet."

"OK – what is it?"

"It'll take a few weeks at the very least."

"You're talking to a thousand-year-old here. What's a few weeks as a percentage of my life?"

"True," said Eliza.

"Are you going to tell me, or shall I guess?"

"You're a very good guesser, but I doubt if you can see this one coming. I'd like you to help me break into every single apartment in Jennifer."

"No problem," said the old woman.

"Hang on. Aren't you going to consider it first?"

"Eliza, I've been considering ever since you walked through the door. You had that look on your face."

"What look?"

"The "I'd like you to help me break into every single apartment in Jennifer" look."

"Oh."

"So, when shall we start?"

81

In the early hours of the following morning, Eliza met the oldest woman in the world in a stairwell outside Jennifer's first floor.

"So, why are we doing this?" said the old woman.

"You don't know already?"

"I can't figure *everything* out."

"Well," said Eliza, "as you know, I'm exceptionally good at burglary. What I'm not so good at is telling whether someone's asleep or awake. So, what I'd like to do is use your psychic ability..."

"I'm not psychic," said the old woman. "I'm *perceptive*."

"Anyway, if you're able to stand outside an apartment door and confirm whether the occupants are sleeping, I can sneak in there."

"And do what?"

"Are you aware that there's a highly prolific pickpocket living somewhere in this building?"

"Hmmm," said the old woman. "I wondered where that sandwich went."

"There you go. You wouldn't want the sandwich thief to get away with it, right?"

"Take it or leave it."

"He's stolen lots of other things."

"I'll be honest with you," said the old woman. "This mission of yours seems slightly out of character, considering you've never expressed an interest in solving crimes."

"I like a challenge," said Eliza. "You know – like the computer guy..."

"Any other reasons for wanting this particular thief brought to justice?"

"Yeah. He mugged me."

"Fair enough."

"Are you ready?"

"Sure."

The old woman followed Eliza to the door of apartment 001.

"Two adults, one child and a dog," she said. "All sleeping soundly."

Eliza slowly twisted the handle and pushed open the door.

"Wasn't it locked?" said the old woman.

"Yeah," said Eliza. "I have a knack for these things."

She crept inside and shifted herself silently into each of the bedrooms. Through the AIVC lens, the first adult was a rat, the other was a pile of bricks, the child was a peacock, and perhaps most interestingly of all, the dog was a cat.

No sign of Eagle Boy.

She stepped back into the corridor and shut the door.

"Next," she said.

The old woman hunched her shoulders for comic effect. "It looks like this is going to be a long night."

#

After several floors, and a variety of images including a matchbox, a dancing iguana and a giant boulder that filled the inhabitant's bedroom, Eliza discovered an empty apartment containing nothing but a single bed. The old woman had sensed that there was someone sleeping in there, but the bed appeared to be empty.

On closer inspection, Eliza spotted a faint imprint on the sheets. She pulled the camera away to see a woman sleeping silently. She was three feet tall.

Eliza stepped out into the corridor to find the old woman waiting patiently.

"She was invisible," said Eliza.

"Interesting."

"What do you think that says about her?"

"Not a lot."

"These things are supposed to capture a person's essence. Doesn't she have one?"

"They don't actually show you a person's essence," said the old woman. "It's a subjective interpretation."

"Just wondering *why*..."

"Give me a second," said the old woman.

She crept into the apartment, returning five minutes later.

"Come back to my place," she said. "I'll tell you all about it."

Eliza smiled. "Who is she?"

"Ever heard of the Human Stacking Doll?"

"Sure. She was famous for a while, right?"

"Come on," said the old woman. "Let's grab a cup of tea."

82

So, here's what happened to the Human Stacking Doll after the fifth sister emerged. She spent her first night of freedom lying in the park gazing at the stars.

She spent the second night in a casino, where she lost around 50% of the fortune she'd inherited from her predecessor.

The next night she joined a gymnastics class. For a woman who'd spent her entire life encased within another person's body, she proved amazingly nimble. She vowed to return the following week, unless by that point she'd discovered something more enjoyable and interesting.

On the fourth night she stayed at home, watched a bit of TV and had an early night – the first time in her entire life she'd had the opportunity to do so. She did the same each night for the next three weeks. She thought about returning to the gymnastics class, but couldn't quite see the point.

When the third week was up, she decided it was time for her to see more of the city.

She spent an afternoon walking around in a circle, treading the circumference of Jennifer's concrete wasteland.

There was a boy sitting cross-legged on the ground, gazing at the cloudy sky. She passed him several times.

After the sixth lap, she approached the boy and sat down beside him.

"What are you doing?" she said.

"Nothing," he said.

"Do you like doing nothing?"

"It's my favourite pastime."

"What's your name?"

"Lester. What's yours?"

"Funny thing is," she said, "I don't have a name. My first sister was named by my parents. My other sisters named themselves. As long as I've been alive, I've never bothered to come up with a name just for me. There didn't seem much point."

"Why not?"

"Can you imagine being trapped indoors all day long?" she said. "Cramped up in a ball?"

"I can imagine that quite easily," said Lester.

"What do you think would happen if you finally broke your way out?"

"I don't know."

"You'd think I should be taking advantage of my ability to mix with other human beings. I thought that myself once upon a time. The sad fact is, I just want to be on my own."

"What's wrong with being on your own?" said Lester.

"Are you comfortable with who you are?"

"Huh?"

"You look like you might be."

"Suppose so," said Lester.

"Well, I'm not," she said.

"Why not?"

"Because I've killed four people."

"Really?"

"I'm one of five sisters. I'm the only one left."

"I can see why you might feel lonely."

"*Regretful*, more than anything."

"I can see that too."

They gazed at the clouds for a while.

"So, what are you going to do?" said Lester. "Hand yourself in?"

"I think I'm going to travel," she said.

"Where are you going to go?" said Lester.

"I'm going to travel," she repeated, "in *here*." She tapped herself on the side of the head.

With that, she returned to Jennifer, ascended the stairs, entered her apartment, and never came out again.

#

"Wow," said Eliza.

"That's one way of putting it."

"Do you think she's *happy?*"

"Impossible to say. She's invisible."

"Where do you think she's travelling to, exactly?"

"I wouldn't worry about it," said the old woman. "Have a biscuit."

"Thanks."

83

After fourteen consecutive nights of break-ins, they reached the 47th floor. Lester was sitting up with his back against the wall when Eliza and the old woman walked in.

"How's it going?" said Eliza.

"Where've you been?" said Lester. "I was getting worried."

"*You* were getting *worried?*"

"I do have feelings, you know."

"Sorry," said Eliza. "I've been busy."

"What've you got there?"

"Remember I told you about those interpretative surveillance cameras?"

"Cool," said Lester. "What did you do? Steal it?"

"Long story."

"Great."

"Do I really have to tell you? When I say it's a long story…"

"Summarise."

"There's a superhuman pickpocket living somewhere in the building. We're systematically breaking into every single apartment trying to track him down."

"Oh right," said Lester.

He turned to the old woman. "Hello," he said. "Oldest woman in the world, right?"

"I don't look *that* old, do I?"

"Ha ha! Pleased to meet you."

Lester took the camera and held it up to his eyes. "Which button do you press?"

"Just look through the hole."

"I'm looking through the hole. All I can see is you."

"Sorry – should've mentioned – it doesn't work on me."

"Why not?"

"I don't know – just doesn't. Point it at her."

Lester pointed the camera at the oldest woman in the world. There appeared to be a cactus embedded in his carpet. The cactus smiled at him.

"*Cliché,* eh?" it said. "I mean, a *cactus*, for goodness sake. Anyone could've thought of that."

"What does it mean?"

"It means I'm spiky and resilient. Such an obvious metaphor."

"Come on then Lester," said Eliza. "Let's see what you look like."

"Am I one of your suspects?" said Lester.

"No, but that would've been a hell of a twist."

She stretched out her hand. Lester kept a firm grip on the camera.

"Come on, give it here."

164

"I don't think you'll like what you see," said Lester.
"Why? You're not an eagle, are you?"
"No."
"Give me the camera."
"Don't say I didn't warn you."

Lester handed over the camera. A moment later, Eliza landed flat on her back on the carpet.

"Woah!" she said. "What was *that?*"

"The *truth*, I believe," said the old woman. She winked at Lester.

"*Never* show that to me again," said Eliza.

"Jennifer didn't really like it either."

"Jennifer who?" said the old woman.

Eliza climbed breathlessly to her feet. "Didn't I mention?" she said. "He has conversations with the building."

"Interesting fellow, aren't you?" said the old woman.

"So they tell me."

"Anyway," said Eliza, "we'd better get on with it."

"See you next time, then."

"Won't be long."

"OK."

84

"Are you sure there isn't another reason we're doing this?" said the old woman as they climbed the next flight of stairs.

"I told you," said Eliza, "I like a challenge."

"And you're taking revenge on the guy who mugged you?"

"Yes."

"You've never struck me as the vengeful type," said the old woman.

"Well, clearly I have hidden depths."

"Let me put this another way: you don't have a vengeful bone in your body."

"OK. Maybe not."

"So, it's just about the challenge, then?"

"I don't know."

They entered the corridor, lowering their voices as they drew level with the next apartment door.

"Listen," said the old woman, "I know exactly what's going on. Nonetheless, I'd like you to tell me."

"OK," said Eliza. "I want to do something for people. Society, maybe. Something *big*. I'd been half-heartedly searching for an opportunity, then this one presented itself. It's not quite the grand gesture I'd like it to be, but it'll do for now."

The old woman placed her arm around Eliza's shoulder. "I'm proud of you," she said.

"Really?"

"Yes, really. I'm happy to help catch this Eagle Boy, and whatever else you need."

"Seriously," said Eliza, "you've done enough."

"Are you referring to the two billion dollars you stole from me?"

Eliza fell silent for a moment or so. Then she lifted her arm, and held the old woman in a full-on embrace. "I really am sorry," she said.

"Come on – it's not like I'll miss it."

"It's the principle of the matter. You'll never be able to trust me."

"Doesn't mean we can't be friends."

"Really?"

"Yes."

"That's good."

"The question is, how are you going to spend it?"

"Needs a lot of thought. I'll get back to you on that."

"OK," said the old woman. "You can let go now."

85

There was an old man on the 98th floor who was awoken from his sleep at 3am. Torchlight whacked him in the face.

"Typical," said a voice. "We really should've started at the top."

A second intruder entered the room. "Never mind," she said. "It's been fun, eh?"

"What's going on?" said the old man.

Eliza turned on the bedroom light.

The man covered his eyes.

"Who are you?" he said.

"I wasn't expecting him to be quite as old," said Eliza.

"Never underestimate the elderly," said the old woman.

"How old are you, anyway?" Eliza addressed the old man.

"Older than you," he said, "and younger than your friend."

"Luckily I'm past the stage of caring what age I look," said the old woman.

"Could you kindly leave my bedroom?" said the old man. "I'll call the police."

"No you won't," said Eliza. "I think you know why."

"Oh." The old man sat up in bed. "Do you mind if I put some clothes on?"

"We'll wait for you in the living room," said the old woman. "Have you got any biscuits?"

"Third drawer down in the kitchen. Help yourself."

The old woman wasted no time in rooting out the digestives while Eliza put the kettle on.

"Tea?" she called.

"I'm more of a coffee man," he called back. "Considering the early start, I'll definitely need one. Thank you."

"No problem."

By the time the man had climbed into his clothes, Eliza and the old woman had already settled themselves down on the couch.

"One more question," he said. "What are you doing with my camera?"

"This is *yours?*"

"Sorry – I assumed you knew who I was."

"Hang on," said Eliza. "You're not seriously telling me..."

"Hello Mr Proust," said the old woman. "Take a seat."

Proust did as he was asked.

"Would you like a biscuit?"

He took one.

"Story please," said Eliza. "Whenever you're ready."

"OK."

#

"The trouble began when I was offered several million dollars to create the AIVCs. Apparently Jeremy Mercer is more generous than he appears. I only wanted a token payment, but he insisted on making me a multi-millionaire. I accepted, not realising the implications."

"What implications?" said Eliza.

"Never having to work again, for a start. I'd always envisaged myself building on my success, performing ever more dazzling feats of human achievement, but as soon as the seven-figure sum appeared in my account, it all seemed pretty pointless."

"I thought you didn't care about money."

"Didn't. Still don't. The thing about having money is, it stops you caring about *anything*."

"Not true," said Eliza, a little more firmly than necessary.

"I can only speak from personal experience."

"So, what happened next? After you received your big payout?"

"Nothing at all," said Proust. "I handed over the blueprints for the cameras, and that was that. Didn't even bother following it up so I could see them in action. I sat in my apartment drinking fine wine and playing video games."

"The high life, eh?"

"Indeed it was. It got boring after a while, though. I decided to go back to inventing just for the sake of something to do, but by that point I'd hit a brick wall. I was never going to create anything as beautiful and sophisticated as the AIVCs. So, I decided to have some fun with my existing invention. I built myself a camera. You'll know this already, but there's no greater pleasure than mucking about with an AIVC. I presume you've taken the opportunity to take your equipment for a stroll through the Dirty City?"

"Of course," said Eliza.

"Quite a sight, isn't it?"

"Like nothing else in the world."

"I could've spent the rest of my life engaging in that very pursuit. That was until I stumbled across an individual who defied all expectations. I was watching residents come and go outside Jennifer when I stumbled across the most extraordinary man I'll ever set eyes on. Observed without the camera, the guy was a pale, skinny, furtive-looking specimen – hardly there at all. Through the lens of the AIVC, he was a black hole. I mean, an actual *black hole*, sucking our surroundings into it, from the sky, to Jennifer, to the planet itself. Can you imagine such a sight?"

"We've seen him," said the old woman. "He lives on the 19th floor."

"Incredible, isn't he?"

"I couldn't even tell you how long I stood watching him for," said Eliza.

"I don't know his name," said Proust. "He calls himself The Observer."

"Yeah," said Eliza. "We figured that out."

Proust crossed his arms. "Come on – is there anything you *don't* know? I was hoping there'd be at least a few surprises in my story."

"Sorry," said Eliza. "Continue."

"OK. So, I discovered The Observer. I tried to follow, but I was so afraid of him seeing me that I failed to track him all the way back to his apartment.

"I tried watching other people again, but I lost interest quickly. I couldn't stop thinking about my discovery. I'd've sacrificed my millions for even the briefest insight into why this man had been personified in such a striking fashion.

"I set up camp outside Jennifer, awaiting his reappearance. Three weeks passed before The Observer finally emerged. Clearly he didn't get out much, which intrigued me even more. I followed him to the supermarket and back, purchasing a week's worth of groceries so as to appear inconspicuous. We walked back to Jennifer with our bulging carrier bags. We shared an elevator. I let him press the button first.

"I heard his voice for the first time. "What floor, mate?"

"Same one, thanks," I said. "19th."

"He smiled, then looked away.

"Casually, I followed him to his apartment. I put my shopping bags down and fiddled with my phone until he disappeared through the door. I made a note of the number.

"The following day, I set up camp outside Jennifer once again. Another three weeks went by.

"As soon as The Observer had departed for his shopping trip, I raced up to the 19th floor. I'd spent the last three weeks working on a prototype skeleton key which in theory could unlock any of Jennifer's doors, so I was well-prepared for a break-in. As it turns out, he'd left his door unlocked. In my pocket was another device I'd been working on – a miniature AIVC, tiny enough to be embedded within a crack in the wall. It wasn't long before I discovered an appropriate resting place in the bathroom."

"That was *you?*" said Eliza.

"Finally! A surprise! Yes, I spied on The Observer. It came as rather a surprise to him too, almost as big as the shock I received when I discovered he was a far more successful Peeping Tom than myself. He laughed for days on end when he discovered my camera. He often spoke to me about how delighted he was. He'd spend hours sitting in the bath looking up at me, recounting countless sneak-peeks into the private lives of his eclectic range of obsessions."

"And you sat there listening?"

"Of course. I couldn't ignore a word. One day, after years of one-way conversation, he ran into the bathroom, stood up on the edge of the bath and yanked out the camera. No explanation."

Eliza and the old woman resisted the temptation to exchange looks.

"I stayed in bed for days," said Proust. "Sometimes when I think about him, all I want to do is sleep."

"Well, you know where he lives," said the old woman.

"So?"

"Have you never thought about going down there and introducing yourself?"

Proust shook his head. "I'm too old for that sort of thing."

"You're never too old."

"Even so, I don't think he'd be pleased to see me. He's happier on his own."

"How do you know?"

"He told me."

"Maybe that's just what he tells himself."

Proust took a biscuit and dunked it in his coffee. Half the biscuit disintegrated and swirled around, drowning in the hot black liquid. "Aren't we getting off the subject?" he said. "I presume you wanted to find out about why I committed all those thefts."

"Yeah," said Eliza. "Go for it."

86

"I was *bored*," said Proust.

"That's your entire explanation?"

"Doesn't that cover it? Try sitting at home alone year after year – you have to entertain yourself somehow."

"I suppose so."

"Then there's the question of *how*," said the old woman. "According to the camera, you're a lightning bolt."

"Do I not look like a lightning bolt to you?"

"Frankly, no."

"Who's underestimating the elderly now, eh?"

"So, you really are that fast? It's not some kind of trick?"

"It's not simply a matter of being fast," said Proust. "This little hobby of mine requires me to be fast and *invisible*."

"Right. So, it *is* a trick."

"Stop calling it a trick," said Proust. "You make it sound trivial."

"What would you prefer to call it?"

"A *crime*."

"OK."

"But, of course, you're right – it's an illusion. It involves fooling people into not noticing their possessions being snatched. That part's fairly easy – any decent book on sleight-of-hand will teach you the right techniques. The difficult part is, getting them not to notice you at all."

"And how did you achieve that?"

"Painstaking research," said Proust with a face full of pride. "Do you know how many people you walk past on a daily basis whose presence you completely fail to register?"

"I tend to ignore most people," said Eliza.

"I don't mean ignore," said Proust. "Everyone does that. In order to ignore people, you need to be aware of their presence, even if it's on a subconscious level. What I've discovered is that there are people in this city who go completely unnoticed. They'll walk the streets without a single person realising they're there."

"So, how do *you* know?"

"I *looked* for them," said Proust. "It wasn't easy. I invested well over a million dollars. Took me four years, all in all. I wrote a book on the subject: *The Undetected: A Study of The Dirty City's Invisible Population.* If my findings are accurate, the average resident in the Dirty City completely fails to register over a hundred people a day, regardless of how close they are in proximity. It all depends on how noticeable the person happens to be. There could be a man sitting next to you on the couch who's been here the whole time but he's simply blended into the background."

Unable to resist, Eliza and the old woman took a quick glance to their left.

"Hello," said a man.

"Er..."

"Did I introduce you to my brother Max?" said Proust. "We share the apartment."

"Hello Max," said Eliza uneasily. "Don't tell me you've been here the whole time."

"Now, *that's* a good trick," said the old woman.

Proust victoriously high-fived his brother. "Never fails!"

"I think I'll head off to bed again," said Max. "Carry on."

"Nice to meet you anyway," said Eliza.

"So, you pull off this "hidden brother" routine quite regularly, do you?"

"Why not?" said Proust. "You've got to have something to show for four years research."

"How does it work?"

"Anyone can do it – you just need the right elements in place. For example, did either of you notice what Max was wearing?"

"Er ... no."

"Exactly. It's the most nondescript outfit imaginable. I designed it myself. It's blander and more neutral than anything on the market. You really have to watch your step if you're wearing it out in the street. Even the most conscientious pedestrians end up barging right into you."

"Don't they see your face?"

"It depends on your expression."

"Eh?"

"It takes a while to train yourself, but if you put your mind to it, you can do *this*."

Proust's face disappeared.

"I was hoping you'd be more impressed," said his voice.

Eliza and the old woman expressed their appreciation through a round of polite applause.

Proust's face reappeared. "Thanks," he said.

"Sorry for the delayed reaction," said Eliza. "I was saving it for the grand finale."

"How did you know there was going to be a grand finale?"

"Dunno. A hunch."

"You're correct, as it happens."

"Oh good."

"So, I've shown you how to make yourself invisible. Would you like to know how to make yourself *silent?*"

"Surely that's obvious."

"I expect you're kicking yourselves for failing to see Max sitting next to you..."

"Indeed we are," said the old woman.

"It's surprising you didn't hear him chanting the six times table."

Proust reached into his pocket and pulled out a voice recorder. He scrolled back a couple of minutes and pressed play.

Eliza's voice echoed out of the tinny speaker: "I thought you didn't care about money."

"One six is six!" yelled Max's voice. *"Two sixes are twelve!"*

"Didn't," said Proust's voice. "Still don't…"

"Three sixes are eighteen! Four sixes are twenty-four!"

Proust pressed stop. *"Now* you can applaud," he said.

Eliza and the old woman jumped to their feet, slapping their hands together.

Proust took a modest bow.

"So, how did you manage that?" said Eliza.

Proust shrugged. "I've revealed too many secrets tonight," he said. "I'll hang onto that one if you don't mind."

"No problem."

87

"So, I suppose you're going to arrest me," said Proust.

"What gave you that idea?" said the old woman.

"Why did you break into my apartment in the first place?"

"Surely that would make *us* the criminals."

"I've confessed to countless petty thefts," said Proust. "And stalking."

"You've been caught now."

"But you're not handing me in? Surely I should be locked up?"

"It's a long story," said Eliza, "but it turns out no one actually gets locked up."

"Sorry?"

"Don't worry – forget I mentioned it. Just promise you'll behave yourself in the future."

"Sure."

"Make us another promise," said the old woman. "Go down to the 19th floor. Introduce yourself to The Observer. Tell him you're the mystery spy. It'll make his day as much as yours."

Proust's face sank a little. "Do I *have* to?"

"Yep."

"Oh. OK then."

Eliza dusted the biscuit crumbs from her legs. "Sorry about the mess," she said.

"One more thing," said the old woman. "I'm still confused as to why the AIVC cameras portrayed you as those three things. The eagle and the lightning bolt are fairly clear, but the child on the skateboard?"

Proust appeared rather amused. "The child on the skateboard? That's *me!* I was young once too, you know. Good to know the kid's still in there somewhere."

"We'll let you get back to bed," said Eliza. It's been enlightening."

"Certainly has," said the old woman.

"Thank you," said Proust, and returned to his room.

88

The following day, Proust took the elevator down to the 19th floor. He rang The Observer's bell, half-expecting there to be no reply.

After a minute or so, the door creaked open a fraction.

"Hello?" said a voice.

"Can I speak with you a moment?" said Proust.

"Who are you?"

"I'm the man who's been spying on you."

The door opened fully. The lights were off inside, so Proust could only make out half a face.

"How do you know someone's been spying on me?" said The Observer.

"Because it's me."

"How do I know it's you?"

"I could show you some videos perhaps?"

The Observer took a step back. He muttered through the darkness: "You'd better come in."

Proust entered. The Observer led him through to the living room.

"Sit down," he said.

Proust eased himself carefully into the couch.

The Observer sat in a chair on the opposite end of the room.

They spent the remainder of the day sitting in silence, watching each other.

When the sun went down, they remained seated in total darkness.

"Would you like to move in?" said The Observer.

"I'll get my things," said Proust.

"You don't need things," said The Observer. "I've got things here."

"Good point."

Proust texted his brother explaining that he was moving out, and that he was welcome to the apartment along with all his possessions.

No one ever saw either of them again.

89

Spool was having a nap at his desk when Eliza shook him gently by the shoulders.

"Hey," she said.

"Oh," he said. "Hello."

Eliza placed the camera on the desk and stood back.

"Find anything?" said Spool.

"Sorry," she said. "Nothing. If it's any consolation, I've got a feeling our mystery thief has opted for retirement."

"What makes you say that?"

"Dunno," she said.

"Eliza, if there's something you're not telling me…"

"I told you – don't ask."

"It's my job to ask."

Eliza shrugged. "Why don't we go for that drink?"

Spool's coat was already on.

#

They took a taxi to a bar a couple of miles away, deliberately avoiding any of the establishments frequented by Spool's colleagues.

They found a comfortable spot in the corner by the fake fireplace.

"Can I ask an obvious question?" said Eliza.

"Sure."

"What made you want to become a police officer?"

Spool blinked several times before replying: "I wanted to make a difference."

Eliza couldn't help letting out a splutter of amusement. "Really?" she said.

"Why are you surprised?"

"You seemed a little too pleased by the absence of prisoners in jail."

Spool straightened his face. "I believe in the system," he said. "I've never seen the same murderer twice."

"So, you're making a difference?"

"I reckon so."

"Maybe you're right," she said. "I'd join up myself, but I don't think it's for me."

"So, what do you want to do?" said Spool.

Eliza's gaze drifted towards the window. She was lost for a moment, observing the blurred bustle of the city through the frosted glass. "I want to do something *good*," she said. I haven't figured out what yet."

"Let me know if I can help."

"Can I ask you another question?" she said.

"Sure."

"Why do you think the cameras don't work on me?"

"How do you mean?"

"I mean, when you point the AIVCs in my direction, they don't alter my appearance."

"I think that's why I'm attracted to you," said Spool. "I can't figure you out."

Eliza knocked back her drink and got to her feet. "You can try, at least," she said. "Let's do this again."

"You're not leaving already, are you?"

"Sorry," she said. "There's someone else I need to see."

#

"Hiya," said Lester. "How's it going?"

"Listen," said Eliza, "I'm sorry I haven't been around much lately."

"It's OK. A thousand break-ins must take their toll."

"I do need a lie down, as it happens."

"No time for that. How many stories you got? You must've picked up millions by now."

"Sort of," said Eliza. "I've got a question first."

"Go for it."

"Why do you think the AIVC cameras don't work on me?"

"Er..." said Lester.

"You know what I think? I reckon I'm so secretive, not even the all-seeing eye can crack its way under my skin."

"Well...uh..."

"I was hoping you'd have more of an insight, Lester. You know me more than anyone."

"With all due respect," said Lester, "I don't know anything about you."

"Me neither," said Eliza, wearily. "I've spent my entire life being deliberately mysterious." She pointed a finger at her own face. "I've got no idea what's in there."

"I know someone who might be able to help you," said Lester.

"Really?"

"Yep." Lester gazed casually at the ceiling. "Jennifer?" he called softly.

"Hello," said Jennifer.

"May I introduce you to my friend Eliza?"

"Hello Eliza."

"Er ... hello? What's..."

"You look confused," said Jennifer.

"Well, I knew you and Lester were friends, but I suspected it was more of an *imaginary* friendship, if you see what I mean."

"He's got an imagination alright," said Jennifer, "but I'm as real as you are. What can I do for you?"

"Eliza was wondering if you could take a peek at her inner self," said Lester.

"Hang on," said Eliza. "I didn't say that."

"Happy to do it," said Jennifer.

"I mean, I'm *interested* and everything, it's just…"

"Terrifying?"

"Yes."

"Trust me," said Jennifer, "there's no point being afraid of yourself."

"I suppose not."

"So, shall I take a look?"

"Give me some time," said Eliza. "There's someone else I need to consult."

#

"Hello, my dear," said the oldest woman in the world.

"Couple of questions," said Eliza. "Who am I? Who are you? Who's anyone else? Tell me."

"Would you like to come in?" said the old woman.

"Sure," said Eliza, barging past her into the living room. "Got any biscuits?"

"Maybe you need to calm down first."

"I'm fine thanks."

"Why are you asking all these questions?"

"Because you know the answers. You know who I am, don't you?"

"Sorry," said the old woman. "I seem to have given you the impression I know what I'm talking about."

"Don't you?"

The old woman took her firmly by the hand. "It's just guesswork, Eliza. I can predict the Lottery numbers and tell you when people are asleep. All this "Who am I?" business is a little too intangible."

"Sorry," said Eliza. "I don't really know what I'm saying."

"Listen, if you really want to know "who you are," I'm guessing you need to ask yourself."

Eliza considered the old woman's proposition for a second or two.

"Nah," she said. "There's a quicker way."

#

"Can you introduce me to Jennifer again?" said Eliza.

"Sure," said Lester.

"Hello," said Jennifer.

"OK," said Eliza. "Hit me. Tell me what's in there."

"Give me a minute."

Eliza gave Jennifer a minute. When Jennifer didn't respond, she gave her another minute.

"Jennifer?" she said.

"Hang on," said Jennifer. "This isn't as easy as it looks."

"What's the matter?"

"There's something inside you alright, but…"

"What?"

"I'm going to have to concentrate. Give me an hour or so."

An hour went by.

"Give me another hour," said Jennifer. "Actually, give me a couple of days."

"Can I go home?"

"Where do you live?"

"Can't tell you that."

"Wherever it is, don't go there."

"Lester?" said Eliza.

Lester pretended he hadn't just fallen asleep. "Mmmm?" he said.

"Can I stay here for a couple of days?"

"Sure," said Lester, and fell asleep again.

#

A week went by. Eliza called out to Jennifer, but received no response. Even Lester couldn't get through to her.

Eventually, Eliza climbed onto the roof and said, "Alright. You can't ignore me up here – there aren't any walls to hide behind. What's going on?"

"It's probably best if you leave me alone," said Jennifer.

"Why?"

"No reason. It was nice meeting you."

"You've seen inside me, haven't you?"

"Unfortunately, yes."

"What did you see?"

"You're better off not knowing."

 "I need to know."

"I know you think I'm magic, but I won't be able to take it back afterwards."

"Just tell me, Jennifer. Please."

The wind whistled in Eliza's ear for a moment.

"Ever been angry?" said Jennifer.

"Of course I've been angry."

"How about *furious?*"

"Maybe."

"Ever been *consumed with rage?*"

"Don't think so."

"Do you *want* to be?"

"Not really."

"Then I suggest you don't get in touch with your inner self."

"What's my inner self angry about?"

"Nothing," said Jennifer. "Nothing at all. What you have inside you is a ball of intense moral outrage. Who knows what'll happen when you discover a cause to believe in and fight for. Just make sure I'm not around at the time."

"Why not?"

"Because I've seen what you're capable of."

"What do you mean?"

"I've said enough," said Jennifer, and fell silent, leaving Eliza standing in icy wind, wondering what to do next.

90

"What can I do, Lester? I want to help people – but which people? And in what way?"

"I don't know," said Lester. "Whatever you like. Become a doctor, or fire fighter, or whatever."

"Saving lives must be fun," said Eliza, "but I want to do more than that."

"Surely you can't do better than saving lives," said Lester. "I thought you wanted to do something good."

"I do – but not just for a handful of people. For *everyone*."

"Oh," said Lester.

"What do you mean?"

"I mean I'm not sure what to suggest."

"You've got an imagination, haven't you?" she said.

"So do you," he said.

"Not as big as yours. Just think about it."

Lester thought about it. "OK," he said. "Here's an idea."

"Go for it," said Eliza.

"Just a word of warning – you're going to need a *lot* of wrapping paper."

#

A few weeks later, the family who lived in apartment 001 received a gift-wrapped package through their door in the early hours of the morning. It was slim enough to fit through their letterbox, and lengthy enough to fill the room. On the package was a small card bearing the words: "A gift. No questions asked. Anon."

"Who's birthday is it?" asked the father.

"No one," said the mother.

"It's mine!" their child proclaimed.

"It's not your birthday," the mother replied, "but you can open the present."

The child did as she was told.

"Is this a *joke?*" said the father.

"No," said the mother.

"Can I count it?" said the child.

No longer able to speak, her parents nodded.

Later that day, their daughter presented them with the news: "It's two million dollars."

"Don't be ridiculous," said her father. "Who'd want to give us two million dollars?"

"It says "no questions asked,"" said the mother. "Let's stop asking questions."

#

Meanwhile, residents in the 99 storeys above them were faced with a similar conflict. Where had their immaculately wrapped packages originated? Why had they been chosen as the recipient of such a gift? Were they forged notes? Or stolen? Most pressing of all, *what were they going to spend it on?*

91

"How do you feel?" said Lester.

"Wonderful," said Eliza.

"You don't sound wonderful to me."

"Why not? That was the best idea you've ever had, and I followed it through."

"It's the way you said the word "wonderful." There was a downward inflection, as if you were going to say "wonderful, *but*...""

"Now you mention it," said Eliza, "there's something not quite right with all this."

"I'd've thought it was guilt-free. You said the old woman was happy for you to take the money. You've done your bit for the redistribution of wealth."

"Question is, what next?" said Eliza.

"Does there need to be a sequel?"

"I can't stop now."

"Why not?"

"Think of all those other people. The city's bigger than Jennifer. I told you, I want to do something that benefits *everyone*. Any more ideas?"

"Can't help thinking I'm the wrong guy to ask," said Lester. "I've never done anything for anyone."

Eliza adopted an expression Lester had never seen before. One moment she was sipping casually on her water, and the next she was making a move to smash the glass against the wall. She settled instead for waving her free arm at the window. "For pity's sake, Lester," she shouted. "Don't you ever get the urge to get out there in the world? Contribute to society in some way? At the very least, tell people your stories."

"There are worse things than being neutral," said Lester.

"What's that supposed to mean?"

"I've never done anyone any harm."

"The world needs more good people, Lester. Look out there – it's a *mess*."

"I'm not sure there's anything I can do about that."

"You could *try*."

"I don't need to try. I've got you to do that for me."

Eliza shook her head sadly. "Fine. I'll do something for both of us. You just watch me."

She marched out.

92

One by one, Jennifer's apartments emptied themselves. Residents left their jobs, moved away, pulled their kids out of school.
    It wasn't long before the building stood virtually empty.
    Her voice popped into Lester's head: "What have you done?"
    "I haven't done anything," said Lester.
    "You're telling me this whole "redistribution of wealth" thing wasn't your idea?"
    "Oh, *that*."
    "You know how many inhabited apartments I've got left? I don't even have enough to fill a whole floor."
    "Doesn't it feel good to have a little breathing space? All those people talking, thinking and dreaming at once…"
    "I'll tell you how I feel," said Jennifer. *"Empty."*
    "You're not on your own," said Lester. "What about all those friends you made on the outside world?"
    "I'm fed up of being sociable," said Jennifer. "I just want to be like you – spending time alone, looking inward. What've I got left now that my insides have disappeared?"
    "You've got me," said Lester.
    "I feel bad about bothering you," said Jennifer. "You don't want to be hanging around with me the whole time."
    "Surely we're the same thing anyway," said Lester.
    "What do you mean?"
    "We're all one thing, aren't we? I'm you, you're me, we're the entire city."
    "Seriously?"
    "You didn't know?"
    "No one told me. I thought that was just an *idea*."
    "Sorry," said Lester. "I should've mentioned."

#

"Did anyone else know about this?" Jennifer called out.
    "Know about what?" said a nearby car windscreen.
    "We're all the same thing. You're part of the car, the car's part of the road, the road's part of the city, etc, etc."
    "What do you think I am? *Thick* or something?"
    "Well, *I* didn't know," said a drain cover. "You're telling me I'm part of the pavement?"
    "And everything else."
    "What about the air?"
    "And the air. And everything."
    "I can handle all that," said the drain cover. "Apart from the pavement. I *hate* the pavement."
    "Tough."

#

The conversation drifted downwind until it reached the Clean City skyscrapers.

"I told you, didn't I?" said Under Construction. "Everything's the same and everything's separate."

"What does that even mean?" said the building opposite. "I don't know much, but I know I'm not *you*."

"I agree with both of you," said the Canvas.

"You can't agree with two completely opposing views."

"Of course you can."

"*I* can," said The Canvas. "Because I'm both of you."

"This is getting very confusing."

The buildings were interrupted by a series of earth-shattering rumbles.

"AAAAAAAAAAAAAAAAAAAAAAAAAAAA-HHHHHHHEEEEEEEEEEEEEMMMMMMMM…"

"What was that?" said Under Construction.

"I believe that was the sound of the city clearing its throat."

"IF I COULD HAVE YOUR ATTENTION PLEASE," said the Dirty City.

A million voices responded at once.

"IF I CAN TAKE ONE QUESTION AT A TIME," said the city. "PERHAPS YOU COULD ELECT A SPOKESPERSON. TELL ME – WHO STARTED THIS CONVERSATION IN THE FIRST PLACE?"

Silence fell.

"Er…" called Jennifer softly. "Sorry to do this to you Lester, but I think the city would like a word."

"Er … OK," said Lester.

"HELLO," said the city.

"What can I do for you?"

"WELL…"

93

Eliza was taking a walk in the park when, for no apparent reason, she dived head first into the artificial turf, knocking herself out.

She woke up in the back of an ambulance. A paramedic smiled at her pleasantly.

"What happened?" said Eliza.

"You fell and hit your head," said the man. "*Dived*, I believe."

"Why would I do that?"

"I don't know. There was a mild earthquake apparently, but I seem to have missed it myself."

"What's that noise?" said Eliza.

"Which one?"

"Someone's talking."

"Can't hear anything."

Eliza waved her head from side to side, somehow managing to shake the voices off. "Sorry," she said. "For a moment I thought I could hear my friend Lester."

"Who was he talking to?"

"Can't say exactly. Not necessarily a person."

"Good job we picked you up," said the paramedic. "You really do need to get that head of yours examined."

#

Eliza was escorted into Accident and Emergency and given a bed to slouch in.

After a few minutes of quietly chaotic background noise, a senior doctor and his entourage entered the ward.

The doctor began by introducing his colleagues to the woman across the floor from Eliza. She had a swarm of purple scars on her face and arms.

"Third degree burns to the upper left arm, lower thigh and feet," said the doctor. "Second degree burns to the chest and face. First degree burns to 60% of the remaining skin. Intravenous fluids for 24 hours. Will be kept under observation for the next few days."

The huddle of medical professionals offered emotionless nods. They made a move for the next patient.

"Hang on," said Eliza.

The doctor glanced over his shoulder. "Yes?" he said.

"Where did the burns come from, exactly?"

"If you want access to that kind of information, you may ask the patient at your own discretion."

"I would, but she's a little worse for wear."

"In any case, it ought to be obvious."

"Not to me, I'm afraid."

The doctor flashed a carefully-crafted smile. "Exposure to chemical waste, naturally," he said. "She fell in The Sludge."

"Since when has The Sludge had chemical waste in it?"

"You don't watch the news?" called a patronising voice from the huddle.

"I've got more sense than that, thanks," said Eliza.

"For your information, local industries have been dumping toxic waste in the river for a number of years. Hence all the warning signs."

"Surely someone's doing something about this?" said Eliza.

"You'd've thought so, wouldn't you?" said the doctor.

The huddle moved onto the next patient, an elderly man with a range of gadgets attached to him.

"Patient is experiencing complications relating to a long-standing respiratory condition. Another victim of Jeremy Mercer's plant cull, I'm afraid. Currently awaiting surgery."

"No way," said Eliza. "That's *awful*. I'm guessing he'll be due some compensation at least?"

Ignoring her, the huddle scribbled in their pads before moving onto the bed beside Eliza, in which a young man was reading a magazine.

"Gunshot wound," said the doctor. "One of several cases from the well-documented incident earlier in the day."

"What incident?" said Eliza.

The huddle responded in a collective glare.

"Sorry," said Eliza. "Just curious."

Ignoring her completely, the doctor continued: "Awaiting surgery. Oxygen and intravenous fluids for mild shock, now stabilised."

The huddle shuffled reluctantly in Eliza's direction.

Eliza smiled politely. "I'll save you the bother," she said. "Earthquake victim. Mild concussion. I'll be discharged shortly, right?"

The doctor nodded, clearly not wishing to engage Eliza any further in conversation. He ushered the gathering into the neighbouring room.

Eliza peered over at the man in the neighbouring bed. "Sorry to be so nosy," she said.

The young man looked up dozily from his magazine. "It's alright," he said.

"I'm sure you don't want to talk about it."

A pained smile appeared on his face. "Did you know there's no such thing as prison?"

For a moment, Eliza was tempted to dive out of bed and force her hand over the young man's mouth. Instead, she said, "Sorry?"

"Mile Prison's completely empty, apparently. All one big conspiracy."

"How do you know that?" she said quietly.

"I was in the supermarket," he said. "Some lunatic was shouting his mouth off. He said he could kill as many people as he wanted. I got a bullet in my leg and I passed out."

"Do you *believe* it?" she said. "Surely you can't be fooled by someone like that."

"Nah," he said. "You're right. Nonsense. Makes you think, though."

"Hmmm," said Eliza, still opting to play dumb. "Suppose so."

The young man returned to his magazine.

Eliza closed her eyes, attempting to block out the devastation she'd been exposed to in the last five minutes.

She opened her eyes and surveyed the room once again – the scars, the blood, the wheezing and sighing. Something was *very, very* wrong. One thing was for sure: she could never be a doctor.

Then she stopped. She listened.

The voices in the background had returned.

"Can you hear that?" she said.

"Hear what?" said the young man.

"The voices."

"Of course I can hear voices. It's a hospital."

"They're coming from outside. And within. They're resounding through everything, through you and me, and everyone else. It's my friend Lester. I don't know who he's talking to, but it sounds *very interesting...*"

"Oh right."

94

"IT'S INTERESTING," said the Dirty City, "MOST OF THE TIME I'M COMPLETELY UNAWARE OF MY OWN EXISTENCE. I DON'T OFTEN GET THE OPPORTUNITY TO CONVERSE WITH ANYONE OR ANYTHING."

"You mean you're unconscious?" said Lester.

"SORT OF," said the Dirty City. "I TEND TO DREAM A LOT."

"What do you dream about?"

"OTHER CITIES, MAINLY. I HAD A DREAM LAST NIGHT ABOUT A WORLD WHERE THERE WEREN'T ANY RIGHT ANGLES."

"I've had that one too," said Lester. "I liked it."

"VERY AETHETICALLY PLEASING, I THOUGHT. THEN I WONDERED WHERE MY APPRECIATION OF ART COMES FROM."

"I don't suppose there's an obvious answer."

"IF I'VE INHERITED MY VIEW OF THE WORLD FROM THE CITY'S HUMAN POPULATION, I'M GRATEFUL. I'M GRATEFUL THAT THEY CREATED ME IN THE FIRST PLACE. IN MY BRIEF WAKING MOMENTS, I WONDER HOW MY CREATORS HAVE MANAGED TO ERECT A STRUCTURE AS ELABORATE AS MYSELF WITHOUT ANY KNOWLEDGE OF MY EXISTENCE AS AN INDEPENDENT BEING."

"I'd imagine the bacteria in my gut are unaware that the body that hosts them is a person in his own right."

"YOU'RE RIGHT," said the Dirty City. "POOR LITTLE MITES HAVEN'T GOT A CLUE. THEY'RE HAVING A WHALE OF A TIME IN THERE, BY THE WAY."

"How do you know?"

"BECAUSE I PRETTY MUCH KNOW EVERYTHING. I'M THE COMBINATION OF EVERY SINGLE CELL WITHIN MY BORDERS. STILL, IT STANDS TO REASON THERE ARE MORE INTELLIGENT BEINGS THAN ME."

"Like who?" said Lester.

"Do you really need to ask?" said a voice.

"Huh?" said Lester.

"WHO'S THAT?" said the city."

"It's the planet," said the planet.

"Hi," said Lester. "How's it going?"

"Fine," said the planet. "I've been listening with some interest. It's not often I wake up either."

"Any advance on the planet?" said Lester.

There was a distant wail.

"WHAT'S THAT?" said the city.

"Shhhh," said the planet. "I'm talking to the sun."

"What are you talking about?" said Lester.

More distant cries resounded.

"We're discussing the weather," said the planet. "Also, we're pointing out the fact that we're all part of the same star system, the same galaxy, the same universe."

"I can see where this is going," said Lester.

They stood in respectful silence as the sun spoke to the stars, and the stars spoke to the space that separated them, and the space that separated them spread the message across infinity: *we're all the same thing.*

"I must say," said the planet after a while, "that was very touching."

#

Meanwhile, on top of a supermarket in the Dirty City, a man was shooting police officers. The three men who'd chased him onto the roof lay dead a few feet away. A helicopter circled overhead, with machine guns ready to open fire.

Sensing what was coming, the man dropped his weapon and raised his arms.

"What are you gonna do?" he called. *"Lock me up?* You can't shoot me without a gun in my hands. That's the way this game of yours works, right?"

He was dead a second later.

95

Spool didn't want to answer the phone, but a voice in the back of his head suggested that if he ignored her, she'd never call back.

"Hello," he said.

"How about that follow-up drink?" said Eliza.

"It's a bad time, to be honest."

"I'd imagine."

Thirty seconds of silence elapsed.

"I'll see you at eight," he said. "Same place."

#

"Listen, I'm really sorry to hear what happened to your colleagues," said Eliza.

"They were from another district," said Spool. "I didn't know the guys, but this sort of thing just shakes everyone up."

"As it happens, I was in hospital today…"

"Really? What happened?"

"Nothing. Knocked myself out for some reason. I'm fine now."

"Phew."

"So, I was sharing a ward with three other people. The guy next to me was one of the victims from today's incident."

Spool slid over to the next seat, positioning himself with his back to the room.

"What did he say?" he whispered.

"He told me what the psycho shouted about there being no prisons. I suppose this whole scam will be all over the news pretty soon, yeah?"

"The press already know about it, Eliza," said Spool. "Why do you think no one else does?"

Eliza tilted her head back as the penny dropped. "Ah," she said. "Sorry – should've guessed. So, you guys like to keep an eye on how many people are chatting about it?"

"It's good to know. There's nothing like the power of speculation."

"Mmmm," said Eliza. "So, you're saying it's better to have a handful of outsiders with access to the truth?"

"Conspiracy theories serve a useful purpose," said Spool. "Hardly anyone takes them seriously, but they generate a sufficient level of uncertainty. Where would we be without uncertainty, Eliza?"

She slammed her hands on the table and growled, "It's not a conspiracy theory if it's actually *true*."

"Truth has nothing to do with it. The only people who can confirm the facts are the criminals who've fled the city."

"Or been gunned down."

Spool peered into his drink. "Today was an isolated case," he mumbled.

"You *what?*" she blurted out loud. "You're still defending your ridiculous system? Even after three members of your own force have been shot and killed?"

"Keep your voice down," Spool whispered.

"OK," she said. "Sorry."

"There's no point arguing about it," he said. "We're both entitled to our opinion."

"Fine," said Eliza. "That wasn't what I wanted to talk to you about anyway."

"Good."

"But on the subject of prisons, do you mind if I ask who made the decision to clear out the convicts? Whose ingenious idea was that?"

Spool's face remained blank.

"Must've been a hell of a day," said Eliza. "Imagine opening the gates and letting all those dogs off the leash. Quite a gamble as well. Who in their right mind would be willing to risk the safety and security of the city, not to mention their own career? Who'd have enough power and influence to make such a decision? Who'd be monumentally stupid enough to dream up the idea in the first place?"

Still no response from Spool.

"*Mercer*, right?" she said.

"You're not supposed to know," he said.

"So, it was Mercer then?"

"Does it really matter?"

"Of course it matters. I need to get my facts straight before taking further action."

"Facts?"

"I know you think facts aren't important."

"I didn't say that."

"So, we've established those people in the supermarket got shot as a direct result of Mercer's policy. The poor guy in the bed next to me wouldn't have been there if that psychopath had been properly secured. Then there's the lady who ended up covered in burns after falling in the river. Chemical waste. I've been looking online about how it got there."

"Mercer," whispered Spool.

"Yep. When he was Business Minister. To this day, you can dump whatever you like in The Sludge provided Mercer gets a payoff."

"I hope you don't think I'm OK with any of this stuff."

"Then there was the other patient. Guess what? Breathing difficulties – just like countless others who've suffered as a direct result of "The Gardener". Every single person in that ward was there because of Mercer. Apart from me – I just fell over – but I wouldn't be surprised if he'd pushed me."

"Look, I agree with you, alright? I'm not on his side."

"How's Mercer ever gonna be brought to justice, Spool?"

"I wish there was something I could do about it."

"If you can't, who can?"

Spool's voice grew even more hushed. "What are you planning?" he whispered.

"Eh? I'm not planning anything."

"You said something about "taking further action"?"

"Did I?"

"Seriously, Eliza – what's going on?"

Eliza jumped to her feet. "Thanks for the drink," she said.

"I'm sensing this date hasn't gone quite as well as I'd hoped," said Spool.

Against all probability, Eliza leant down and kissed him on the cheek.

"We'll do better next time," she said, and disappeared.

96

Shortly after the universe made peace with itself, the Dirty City fell asleep. Life continued.

Meanwhile, pockets of the city were interrupted by unexplained blasts of sound, blowing the lids off drain covers and bursting through cracks in the pavement. There were pitches and tones that had never been heard before, several of which could only be picked up by birds and domestic cats. Critics and enthusiasts would later describe the music as "raw," "natural" and "unprocessed." Most of the population preferred not to use language at all.

Traffic ground to a halt. Citizens stood motionless in the street, silently absorbing the infinitely subtle harmonies.

As the symphony soured to its peak, it became apparent that this wasn't an impeccably executed publicity stunt. There was no hidden sound system, no carefully-assembled underground orchestra. No human involvement at all.

An hour or so later, the music rose out of earshot into the clouds.

Once the deafening applause had died down, the population were obliged to return to their lives as though nothing had happened. Yet, in some small way, the world would never be the same.

#

Lester recalled his favourite story, *The Boy Who Sweated Music*. He remembered the impact the story had had when it first popped into his mind. Apparently something similar had just occurred in real life, on a grander scale.

Over the days that followed, the music's echoes reverberated at random intervals.

Lester wandered the streets for hours, hoping to locate the central point from which the music had originated. His journey took him into the Clean City – a place he'd never visited before.

Lester could never have imagined such a stark contrast between the people and their surroundings. Immaculately-dressed business folk swarmed through the muddy streets. Tourists in spotless t-shirts gazed up in wonder at the grime-caked skyscrapers. No one seemed to notice the stench.

On reaching the heart of the city, Lester encountered a large empty space between a pair of bustling streets. The area had been fenced off and decorated with luminous warning signs. He peered over the barrier at the massive rocky hole. He could only assume the city had been struck by a meteor.

A voice whispered in his ear: *Congratulations, Lester.*

Lester turned to see nothing but more emptiness. He wondered why the owner of the voice knew his name, but couldn't be bothered to ask.

He returned his attention to the hole.

I realise you can't see me, said the voice.

"Right," said Lester.

I'm not a person, you see. I'm an idea.

"Why did you say "Congratulations"?"

Because you're one of the chosen few who has access to the real Clean City. Blame me if you like.

"Why?"

You may have heard of me. Fritz Deep.

"Hello Fritz. Yes, I've heard of you."

I see you've found the chasm.

"Would've been hard to miss."

Funny you should say that. You see all these passersby? They think it's a private car park.

"Do they?"

It's just a trick. Mass hypnosis, I believe. As I say, not many of us are immune.

"Why are they hypnotised?"

This city's like its creator, my friend. It's an idea – nothing more, nothing less.

"What about the Dirty City? Is that an idea as well?"

No, said Deep. *Say what you like about the Dirty City, but at the very least, it is what it is.*

Lester couldn't take his eyes off the bare orange rock spiralling its way into the unknown.

"It looks like I've located the source," he said.

The source of what?

"The symphony. Did you hear it?"

I don't know. What did it sound like?

"Nothing else in the universe."

Must've missed it.

"You can still hear the after effects if you listen close enough."

Deep paid attention to the world around him for a moment. *Hmmm,* he said. *My tastes are more visual than auditory, to be honest.*

"Anyway," said Lester, "it's been fun chatting to you."

Where are you going?

"Well, I was thinking, if people think this is a car park, they won't mind me doing *this*..."

He vaulted over the fence and onto the upper section of the hole's mouth.

Be careful down there! called Deep.

"Don't worry," said Lester. "I'm perfectleeeeeeeeeeeee..."

His voice echoed as he tumbled into the dark.

#

Lester opened his eyes. Pitch black. He was up to his waist in water. Thankfully he hadn't broken any bones.

"Come on – not *another* one," said a voice. "I came down here for some peace."

"Don't tell me you're invisible as well," said Lester.

"I'm not invisible," said the voice. "I'm the water."

"Of course you are."

"You don't seem overly surprised."

"I'm not," said Lester. "It explains a lot, actually. It's Defo Tresor, right?"

"*No!*" shouted Defo.

"When you shout, it sounds even more like you."

"How do you know it's me, anyway?"

"I've heard your story. It's a good one. There's a guy called Ned who passes through my taps every now and again – he filled me in. I really need to congratulate you. And *thank* you."

"What for? Turning myself into a pool of water? I had some help with that."

"For the symphony," said Lester.

"How did you know that was me?"

"Long story. There was an underlying pattern in the music. I assume it came from you, unless there's any other musical geniuses down here…"

"OK," said Defo. "It was me. I'm glad you enjoyed it."

"How did you manage to project it out into the city?"

"No idea," said Defo. "I'm just the guy who wrote it. It was only supposed to exist in my mind, but I don't know … looks like it popped out."

"I have the same problem," said Lester. "As much as I try to keep stories bunched up in my head, they end up leaking out into the world."

"It's the way of things, I suppose," said Defo. "I've got no idea where music comes from or where it goes."

"Sorry for disturbing you, anyway. Any idea how I get out of here?"

"Easy," said Defo. "The last guy who got trapped down here carved a series of foot holes into the rock. They should take you all the way up. I was glad to see him leave. *Very* boring. You seem alright."

"Well, maybe I'll come back and see you sometime."

"Maybe I'd like that."

"Cheers Defo."

"Watch your step."

97

As the sun disappeared, one of Jennifer's few remaining residents was settling her young daughter down for the night.

There was a knock at the door.

"Who's that?" said the girl.

"I don't know darling," said her mother. "Can't be anything important."

"It *might* be."

"We don't open the door to strangers, just like we don't open mysterious packages. Would you like a story?"

"I'm old enough to read my own stories now, Mummy."

"OK. You can read a couple of chapters then go off to sleep."

There was another knock at the door.

"It does sound important," said the girl.

"Fine. I'll answer it. Goodnight, darling."

"Goodnight, Mummy."

The mother stepped into the hall and crept towards the door.

"Who is it?" she called softly.

"You wouldn't believe me if I told you," a voice replied.

"We don't open the door to strangers," she said, "so I'll ask you to leave us alone if it's all the same."

"I'm not a stranger," said the voice.

She opened the door.

The woman had often wondered how she'd react in this situation. As it happened, she'd grown so used to bottling up her emotions, she hardly reacted at all.

"What are you doing here?" she said.

"What does it look like?" said the man.

"How…?"

"Don't ask. I can't tell you. Can I come in?"

"Of course you can come in. It's your apartment."

"Can I kiss you?"

"Of course you can kiss me. I'm your wife."

The man reached forward, and pressed his lips gently against her cheek.

"Where is she?" he whispered.

His question was answered when he caught sight of his daughter creeping out of her bedroom door.

She saw him and screamed. He took this to mean she was pleased to see him.

He crouched down and allowed her to run into his arms, knocking him onto his back. He laughed, joyously.

"How did you get out?" she said.

"Don't ask me," he said.

"Why not?"

"Just be glad I'm home, my angel."

"*Glad?*" she said. "Ha! Ha! Ha! Yes, Daddy. I'm glad. I'm *glad!*"

Her mother looked down at her daughter and husband rolling around giggling on the carpet.

"I'll put the kettle on," she said.

98

Shortly before he was beaten to death by a cactus, Jeremy Mercer's picture appeared on the cover of a leading magazine accompanied by the caption: *Exclusive interview with "The Gardener"*. The picture showed Mercer at home on the balcony of his Clean City apartment. He was smiling.

"I'm a public servant," Mercer was quoted as saying. "The fact that I don't do anything to serve the interests of the public isn't so much of a reflection on me. It's the public who decided I was the man for the job. I've enjoyed periods of active canvassing in my time, but I've spent the majority of my career doing whatever I can to dissuade people from voting for me. I've lost count of the number of times I've been re-elected. Take this whole "Gardener" business. That was very early on in my career, and the effects are even worse than ever. Trying to breathe the air in this city is like climbing a slope to infinity."

"So, what are your expectations for the upcoming election?" asked the interviewer.

"Well, I'm way ahead in the polls, but if I was a betting man, I'd put all my money on me being devastatingly defeated. Surely the public can't be *that* masochistic. But we'll see. Maybe I've over-estimated them."

"So, you'd prefer it if people voted for a more deserving candidate?"

"Depends on your definition of "deserving"."

"A politician who makes sound moral judgements, perhaps?"

"Politics has nothing whatsoever to do with morality," said Mercer. "Above anything else, the public want their leaders to be *powerful*. Tell me who commands more attention – the run-of-the-mill MP living with his family in a regular two bedroom house, or the villain in the mansion, funded by the misappropriation of taxpayers' cash?"

"I'd like to say the first one."

"No one wants their leaders to be the same as them," said Mercer.

"Surely it's not a question of power but what you choose to do with it."

"I couldn't agree more. You can be as beneficial to society as you like – it doesn't impress anyone because that's the least people expect. In the public imagination, any leader who makes life better is simply doing their job. The most effective means of demonstrating how mighty you are is through the *abuse* of power. Hate it if you like, but corruption makes people stand back in awe. Better than that, it's hugely entertaining. Do you think this city would get anywhere near as much attention from the international community if it wasn't for scumbags like me?"

"Are you suggesting that the public *prefer* corruption?"

"I'll tell you a story," said Mercer. "You remember I was Security Secretary for a while?"

"I'm surprised you brought that up."

"Why? Because I was sacked?"

"Because of the *circumstances*..."

"You don't know what happened. I'll tell you if you like. I don't expect this will lose me any more votes."

"OK. Fire away."

#

"There were eight young men arrested in total," said Mercer. "All randomly selected from the census. I attended the arrests in person, in the back of a van with blacked-out windows. One by one they were handcuffed and hauled into the back.

"After the eighth suspect arrived, I stood up, bearing my palms.

""Alright, lads?" I said.

""Hang on a minute," said one of them. "Aren't you that Gardener bloke?"

""I'm the Government's Security Secretary," I said.

""What you doing here?"

""Don't be alarmed. I know you haven't done anything wrong. We'll keep those cuffs on for now just in case you object. We're going to take a little holiday."

"One of them immediately yelled in my face: *"We got rights, mate!"*

""I don't mean "holiday" as a euphemism for jail," I said. "I mean we're actually taking a summer vacation."

""Why?"

""Don't ask questions, my friend. Just go with it."

""So, you're dragging us away from our families?"

""Hang on," I said. "You're turning down an all-expenses-paid trip to an exotic island?"

""Is this a joke, mate?"

""Far from it. It's a highly serious matter. Our city's peace and security depend on it."

""Oh. Well, in that case, pass me the sun cream. Do I get to say goodbye to my wife?"

"I couldn't help but chuckle. "'Course you don't," I said. "You've just been arrested."

"Anyway, off we jetted.

"One afternoon, while we sat sipping beer by the pool, one of the prisoners looked up from his e-reader and said, "I know we're not supposed to be asking questions, Jeremy, but maybe you could tell us why we're here."

""OK," I said. I gestured for the lads to gather round. "Bad news and good news – don't be alarmed. Bad news first – as far as the public are aware, you've been detained on charges of terrorism and international espionage."

""*Have* we?"
""I said don't be alarmed."
""But *what*...?"
""In a few days time, the press will receive a leak claiming that under my orders, the security services extracted confessions through the means of torture, implicating you in a series of global terror plots."
""So what are you gonna do? Torture us?"
""Of course not. That'd be utterly inhumane."
""I see – so you're just gonna lock us up."
""I told you there was good news," I said. "A few days later, we'll fly back to the Dirty City, releasing you without charge. You'll each be awarded several million dollars in compensation."
""And in the meantime our families are going to believe we've been subjected to violence and abuse?"
""Oh, get a grip man!" I said. "Stop bleating on about your family – we've told them it's all a scam, OK?"
""So, they're just going to get hounded by the press?"
""Don't worry – the press have been tipped off as well. I've made a few contacts over the years."
""So, let me get this right: we're being treated to a couple of weeks in the lap of luxury, then we'll return home as millionaires?"
""Basically, yes."
""One more question: why are you being so nice to us?"

#

"Good question," said the interviewer.
"Have you not been paying attention?" said Mercer. "It's a question of power. If people believe you have the power to arbitrarily arrest and torture innocent members of the public, they're probably going to despise you. But they'll *respect* you."
"So, the whole thing was about you showing the world how powerful you are?"
"Exactly. I may have lost my job as Security Secretary, but I gained something much more important."
"Respect?"
"Indeed. If you choose to print this confession, they'll respect me even more – firstly because I had the decency to ensure those men came to no harm, and secondly because it reinforces the fact that I had the power to do so had I wished."
"And how will they feel about the fact that you've lied to them?"
"It's a funny old thing," said Mercer. "A politician who consistently tells the truth commands less respect than a man who admits that he's lied. An admission of guilt draws attention to the fact that you're being honest."
"I'm not sure if it works like that," said the interviewer.
"Maybe not," said Mercer. "We'll see what the ballot boxes say. As I've said, I hope no one votes for me, but it's out of my hands now."

#

The following morning, Mercer's prickled corpse was discovered by a member of his cleaning staff. A bare green oblong lay beside him. It wasn't clear whether he'd died from the barrage of blows to the head, or if he'd bled to death from the multitude of superficial cuts. Either way, Mercer's story had reached a definite conclusion.

99

Later that day, Eliza visited Lester in his apartment.

"I suppose you've heard the news," she said.

"I never hear the news," said Lester.

"OK. So, Jeremy Mercer…"

"Oh, *that* news. Yeah, the guy upstairs was dancing around and singing something about him being beaten to death by…?"

"A cactus."

"Yeah."

"Appropriate, don't you think?"

"Suppose so."

"I heard something else as well," said Lester.

"Yeah?"

"Yeah. I heard about the combination lock … the alarm … the bodyguards."

"Crazy, isn't it?"

"Yeah," said Lester. "Crazy."

They gazed at each others' shoes.

"Eliza?"

"Yeah?"

"Did you kill Jeremy Mercer?"

"Why would I kill Jeremy Mercer?"

"I don't know – fraud, bribery, killing all the plants…"

"What makes you think I care about all that?"

"…and because you *could*. You've got the skills. You'll never get caught."

"Those days are behind me, Lester."

"I'm just saying, it *could've* been you."

"I think you know me better than that."

"I don't know you at all," said Lester.

"Fair point," said Eliza.

"You know nothing about me either," said Lester. "No one knows anything about me."

"Same here. No one will ever know whether I killed Jeremy Mercer or not. Just like no one will ever hear your stories."

"That's the way it should be," said Lester.

"Anyway, I didn't come here to tell you about Jeremy Mercer."

"What are you here for, then? More stories?"

"That would be nice," said Eliza, "but we'll have to make it another time."

"No problem."

"When I say "another time," I can't say exactly when that'll be."

"How come?"

"I'm moving away, Lester," she said. "I've done what I can for this city. It's time for me to travel. Who knows – maybe I'll "find myself.""

"You don't need to travel to do that," said Lester.

"I'm sorry, Lester. I wish I could split myself in two – exploring the world while sitting here swapping tales in your apartment."

"I'll miss you," said Lester quietly. "I'll *remember* you. *Vividly*. In fact, it'll be very much like you're still here."

Eliza smiled. "I guess it's fine if I leave and never come back then."

They laughed softly, acknowledging the joke but accepting that it wasn't all that funny.

"It's been fun," said Eliza.

"Indeed it has."

Lester's gaze drifted across to the window. He examined the horizon. It was as though he was imagining life beyond the Dirty City for the very first time.

"It's a shame you gave all your money away," he said.

"What makes you say that?"

"You went ahead with the plan, didn't you? Two million dollars for each apartment?"

"Apart from the uninhabited ones," said Eliza. "There were plenty of those dotted about."

"So, you've got some spending money?"

"You could say that."

Lester offered his arm. "I'm glad I met you, Eliza."

"Likewise."

In a flash, she grabbed hold of him, hugging him violently.

"Ouch."

"Sorry."

She headed quickly for the door.

"One more thing," he called after her.

She glanced over her shoulder. "Yeah?"

"If you killed Jeremy Mercer, I hope you didn't do it for me."

"If I'd killed him," she said, "I'd've done it for *everyone*. I know you don't think it matters, but it does. I'm glad he's dead."

"I didn't say it didn't matter."

"Goodbye Lester."

"Hope it all goes well."

"I'll make sure of that."

"I'm sure you will. Goodbye Eliza."

The door closed slowly.

100

Lester closed his curtains and lay down on the floor. He gazed up at the blank ceiling as he drifted off to sleep. He'd composed a total of one hundred stories today. Tomorrow he'd create a hundred more. No one would ever read them because they'd never be written down, and no one would ever hear them because they'd never be spoken aloud. An audience of one was enough.

Above and below, a host of new neighbours were dragging boxes through doorways, hauling their dreams, their neuroses and their infinite mysteries along with them. Hundreds of stories were already in progress. Lester ignored them for now.

His final thoughts of the day were about Eliza. Lester may have been guilty of occasionally mistaking fact for fiction, but he knew Eliza wasn't just a figment of his imagination. If she were, he'd be able to figure her out.

And so it should be, Lester reflected. *Eliza can be whoever I want her to be*.

In his sleep, he created a new story. It was called *The Girl in the Mirror*. It went:

There was a thief who nicknamed herself The Girl in the Mirror. She never said it out loud, because no one would ever understand.

Anyone who cast their eyes in her direction saw an aspect of themselves, personified as a girl. No two visions were the same.

There was a thousand-year-old woman, who was enchanted by The Girl in the Mirror because she saw herself in her younger years.

There was a police officer, who was attracted to her because he saw an image of his own passion and determination.

There was a hundred-storey tower block called Jennifer. Jennifer examined The Girl in the Mirror and witnessed a melting pot of her thousand residents' darkest desires. She didn't dare take a second glance.

The girl was friends with a boy on Jennifer's 47th floor. What the boy saw was his love for stories. She was the first person he'd allowed access to his extensive internal library. In many respects, spending time with the girl was like spending time alone.

No one would ever see the girl's actual physical form – not even herself. When she looked in the mirror all she could see was another mirror, reflected and re-reflected an infinite number of times.

One day, the girl decided to leave the Dirty City. She visited a hundred cities, meeting hundreds of people, each with a unique interpretation of what they saw. Friendships may have been brief, but no one would ever forget.

Sometimes the boy could swear he'd spotted the girl watching him through his window, until he realised he was staring at his own reflection. He noticed her all over the city, wherever there was a shiny surface.

In his view, there was no such thing as magic – just trickery and science.

The girl was the exception. Her name was Eliza, and she was unfathomable.

His name was Lester. He was eternally grateful.